Writings from Moorabool Writers' Craft 2017

Writings from Moorabool Writers' Craft 2017

Moorabool Writers' Craft

Published in Australia in 2017 by;
Trenwick House Publishing.
www.trenwickhouse.com.au

ISBN 978-0-9923514-5-8 (paperback)

Compiling Editor; Kathy Whye
The articles in this anthology were edited by the members of Moorabool
Writers' Craft.

Produced by;
Lightning Source

National Library of Australia Cataloguing-in-Publication entry
Title: Writings from Moorabool writers' craft 2017 / Kathy Whye,
 compiling editor ; Cecilia Clark, Illustrator.

ISBN: 9780992351458 (paperback)

Subjects: Australian literature--Victoria--Moorabool.
 Australian poetry--21st century.
 Short stories, Australian--21st century.

Other Creators/Contributors:
 Whye, Kathy, editor.
 Clark, Cecilia, illustrator.

Foreword

The Writers' Craft project began in 2014 when a group of residents in the Moorabool Shire, Central Victoria, Australia, decided to set up monthly meetings to encourage and support their passion for writing. This anthology represents the rich and diverse creative talent of the group.

We appreciate the guidance by local speakers as well as those from publishing houses and Writers Victoria. They provide invaluable assistance and guidance for our commitment to improving our writing and editing skills. We also thank the Moorabool Shire Council and its Librarians for their support.

While we are inspired to write in different genres with an aim to either self publish or have our work accepted and published professionally, we present this anthology – ***Writings from Moorabool Writers' Craft*** – simply for your enjoyment.

Cover art by Cecilia Clark with respectful acknowledgement of the elements which connect it to the previous anthology cover by artist Caitlin Hogan.

Contents

Wayne Marshall

Wayne Marshall is an Australian writer and musician. Previous work of his has appeared in *Going Down Swinging*, *Writers Bloc*, *Seizure*, *Tincture Journal* and *Gingerbread House*.

Bruce

We're just a small country town—nothing ever happens here. Although there was that one time a shark showed up in our public swimming pool. We called him Bruce, fed him BBQ chickens from the IGA up the road. For a while all the kids in the area held their eighteenths on the grass by the pool, drinking and dancing while Bruce's jagged fin swam laps of the deep end. When that ran its course, local fishing enthusiast Stumpy Taylor took to scaling the fence in the middle of the night and casting a hook baited with marinated steak into the pool. Bruce ignored it and ignored it, until one night he had enough and tore the rod—fisherman and all— into the water, ripping Stumpy's left arm clean off and giving him the nickname we all love and know him by today.

We stayed away from the pool after that, admiring Bruce for his take-no-shit attitude, but knowing he'd overstepped the mark. Seasons went by. Years. The surface of the pool became a rolling swamp of mauled birds. The lawn beside it grew tall and feral. We figured Bruce was lonely. But by god we were lonely too.

And so life went on, until one Good Friday Len Keeley's boy went riding through town shouting Bruce had gone belly-up. We all rushed over for a look. Sure enough, Bruce had gone belly-up. For a moment we stood in silence, heads lowered, admonishing ourselves for taking so little care of the one interesting thing that had come our way in at least a decade. But then there was the beep-beep-beep of a truck reversing, and we all hopped out of the way as Jimmy Smeaton leapt from the driver's side and scrambled through the tall grass, his forehead dripping sweat as he winched the shark from the water and hauled him back along Main Street to his shop, where Bruce presides, still, to this day, a once wild thing reduced to a taxidermied head on a menu board, staring down on us every time we open the door to Jimmy's and step inside to pick up our fish 'n' chips.

[First published in *Seizure*]

Our Year Without Footy

From the moment the sky above our town filled with what looked like a fleet of high-tech sailing ships one morning, and then, from rope ladders tossed over the sides, an army of Fish-Men in spacesuits hurried down and descended on our streets, we knew we were in trouble. It was the end, surely.

Still, we had to be brave. So a bunch of us organised to leave our houses and go confront the invaders. When eventually we found them waiting for us in the middle of Main Street, we approached them slowly, mumbling words of peace and surrender. The leader of the Fish-Men stepped forward. Behind the screen of his helmet, his slimy orange lips flapped open and closed, as if he was speaking to us. Next thing he was pressing a button on his spacesuit and a computerised voice that sounded a lot like the Stephen Hawking voice was translating his words to us: 'No football. One year. Mind experiment. On this town. No football.' His beady eyes blinked rapid-fire. 'Understand?'

'No footy?' we asked, bewildered. 'For a year?'

'No football,' the Fish-Man answered.

'That's it?'

He nodded. 'No football. One year.'

'Or else what?' one of our men asked.

'No remorse,' said the Fish-Man, levelling a silver ray gun at us.

* * * * *

We should probably tell you that footy is a big thing in our town—a massive thing, a colossal thing. Whenever we're not watching it, we're playing it, and whenever we're not playing it, we're thinking about it, and whenever we're not thinking about it, odds are it's cricket season. Going without our favourite sport would be tough. All things considered though, it was as if we'd won the lottery. The creatures weren't going to butcher us and ship us off as exotic meat for the Fish-People back home; all we had to do, for some baffling reason, was go a year without footy. We could do it. Besides, at least initially, we were too swept up in the drama of our visitors to miss footy all that much. We had alien boats bobbing up and down in the sky above our houses, for god's sake. We had men with the faces of fish wandering our streets, filming us, tearing down all footy-related memorabilia from our walls, slapping electrodes on us and showing us images of footballs and goal posts and Four'n Twenty pies mixed with stock war footage and hardcore pornography.

But wonder at the unknown and the thrill of having dodged what appeared to be certain death are one thing. Footy, as everyone in our town will tell you, is another kettle of fish altogether. So it was inevitable that sooner or later one of us would get desperate.

It happened around a month into the occupation. Fifty-two-year-old Ronny Charman had invited four mates to his house on Station Road, where, in the cobwebbed back corner of his shed, he'd hooked up a portable TV to watch a Collingwood versus Carlton match. For the first quarter-and-a-half the men huddled around the television, feasting on the game like drug addicts after a forced withdrawal. They were enjoying it so much that they didn't notice the Fish-Men assembling in the window. When they finally realised they had company—it wasn't until an ad break—the Fish-Man at the front lifted his ray gun and liquidated Ronny Charman. His friends backed away slowly from the TV, their trembling hands held high. Only, they made the mistake of looking back to the screen to see if the Collingwood full-forward nailed his set shot on goal from the boundary.

The men were liquidated immediately, without remorse.

* * * * *

After the murders we had no choice but to banish all thought of football from our minds. But the question was: without footy, what the hell were we going to do with ourselves? We honestly had no idea. So, like a flock of lost sheep, we drifted aimlessly through our days: eating without enthusiasm, going to bed early, sleeping late. During that period it was common to see us parked along the fence line of our footy ground, where we'd sit for hours, staring from the grass to the goal posts to the muddy centre square, pining for a return of the great love of our lives. All the while, the curved bottoms of the boats floated in our windscreens, mocking us, taunting us.

April blurred into May. May was swamped by the dark clouds of June. Giving up any hope that the Fish-Men might buckle and allow us even the smallest dose of footy, we had no option but to let go of the sport altogether. And that's when it happened.

Honestly, you wouldn't believe the kind of changes that came over us. Without footy using up every ounce of their mental and physical energy, our men made up for the years and decades of being half-arsed partners, sweeping wives and girlfriends off their feet. Our collective intelligence skyrocketed. We invented things. We learned foreign languages. We held symposiums in the pub to discuss the future of our post-sport society. A number of us even took up musical instruments, holding impromptu jams on front

lawns and nature strips. These changes seemed to please
the Fish-Men, who stood filming us on the opposite sides of
streets, their gills sucking in and out excitedly, their beady
eyes charged with curiosity and pride.

* * * * *

It wasn't long though before footy was worming its way
back into our collective psyche. Some of us have suggested
that its return was inevitable, natural even. Others have
argued that the Fish-Men's experiment was growing stale,
so without us knowing it they re-introduced the concept of
footy to our minds. This theory is supported by a group of five
wives, who all claim to have woken in the night to find Fish-
Men leaning over their sleeping husbands, playing footy club
songs in their ears, dabbing goanna oil beneath their noses,
dragging red Sherrin footballs provocatively across their
private parts. Either way, as eye-opening as it had been, we
found ourselves becoming restless in our lives without footy.
Yet with the threat of liquidation hanging permanently over
our heads, we knew that if we were to reclaim our beloved
sport, it would have to be covert.

The first meeting was held at the beginning of August,
at the back of our abandoned brickworks factory, in the
middle of the night. We had no actual footballs—the Fish-
Men confiscated every last one of them the day they arrived—
so we milled about in the knee-high grass, unsure what to do.
Ten minutes passed. Then twenty. We were about to give up
and go back to bed when one of us bolted suddenly from the
pack, ran twenty metres ahead, turned, and snapped a right
foot kick back towards the group. At first no one moved. The
only sound was the beep and hum of the boats. But then,
compelled by a force so strong they couldn't resist, the group
leapt as one. At the back one of our smaller men rode on the
shoulders of the pack and took a high-flying screamer of a
mark. No sooner had he hit the ground than he shot off a

handball to a woman on the move. She in turn handballed to her husband, who sprinted, imaginary ball in hand, by the ivy-thick wall of the factory, before stabbing a low pass to his mate on the far side of the paddock. He sent off a quick handball to his neighbour, who from long range slotted a goal between the branches of two gum trees.

And so The Game was born.

Night after night, in unchecked corners of our town, more and more of us gathered in secret to play games of footy that often stretched all the way to dawn. One minute we'd be way out by the strawberry fields, using bits of farming equipment as goal posts. The next we'd be bolting in waves across the green of our bowls club, chasing the player with the ball in his or her hands, trying to lay a tackle or pick up a cheap handball receive. The next we'd be dodging washing lines and yapping dogs, as our matches spilled eventually into backyards. Obviously at some level we were aware that The Game was leading us into dangerous territory, but we followed it, wherever it took us, until one night at the end of August we found ourselves suddenly in the no-go zone beneath the boats. We knew we were in danger, a whole lot of danger, but we played on, kicking and handballing and then kicking again, right into the centre of the field, until finally a handball was fired into the hands of our mayor, who, with dawn breaking through the trees and magpies warbling all around us, barrelled home a goal between two swaying rope ladders. We came from all directions to dive on him, jubilant, red-faced, spent.

When we looked up we saw the entire fish-faced army had us surrounded.

* * * * *

An hour later we were teetering fifty feet above the ground, on the edge of a long metal plank that extended from one of the boats, having been herded up there on a rope ladder at gunpoint. Way down below, those not involved in The Game were beginning to gather as news of our capture spread quickly through the town. At our backs, on the deck, a band of scowling Fish-Men had ray guns trained on us.

'You knew the rules,' rang out the Stephen Hawking voice from the leader. 'And you broke them. Now you must take it. The long walk. Go.'

It was then, for the first time in our lives, that we began to question our relationship with footy. Were we really about to plummet fifty feet and be squashed like bugs because of our obsession with a stupid game? Really? For a second it seemed like the most futile and pathetic death imaginable. But then we came to our senses and realised that if we were going to die—which of course we all are—it may as well be for the greatest bloody game ever conceived in all human history.

'Go,' the leader waved us on. 'Walk the plank. Or be liquidated.'

We joined hands and closed our eyes. We drew our final breaths.

'Liquidate them,' instructed the leader. 'Liquidate them now.'

And then we jumped.

We'd barely fallen a metre before a giant trawling net swung out and caught us. Rocking side to side, we looked up to see the scaly face of the leader, looming at the edge of the plank. For a good minute his furious orange lips snapped at us. Yet when he pressed the button on his spacesuit, all the voice said was: 'No football'.

'No worries,' we shouted back, falling suddenly away from him in the net.

* * * * *

We didn't dare try anything after that. For one, the Fish-Men upped their surveillance, installing microscopic cameras in our walls and commandeering a police car for a 24/7 patrol. Secondly, with only a month of the footy season left to go, we were too close to the end to risk landing ourselves on that god-awful plank again. There was only one problem: the final month was September, and September, as any footy fanatic will tell you, is hands down the greatest month to be alive, as the finals roll into action.

You should've seen us. We were like kids robbed of Christmas. We could almost hear the sound of miracle goals being kicked and drunken spectators roaring in the stands, out beyond the borders of our town. By grand final day we were climbing up the walls. It was a belter of an afternoon too—twenty-nine degrees, not a cloud in the sky—but we gutted it out, hour by hour, minute by minute, until finally the sun was going down on another grand final day. Almost immediately, the Fish-Men were spotted leaving our streets and boarding their ships, preparing, we assumed, for their long journey home now the experiment was over.

As for us, with the footy season done and dusted, we wasted no time turning to the other great sporting obsession of ours.

Have we mentioned yet that cricket is a big thing in our town? No? Well you'd best bloody believe that cricket is a big thing in our town. Whenever we're not watching it, we're playing it, and whenever we're not playing it, we're—

But you get the idea.

The morning after grand final day, with the Fish-Men still up in their boats, we raided our sheds and pulled out all our bats, pads, helmets, stumps and balls. Then, in a show of community solidarity, and to celebrate the great ordeal we'd survived, we packed our cricket gear into bags, collected our deck chairs, stocked our eskies with all the beer and Breezers we could carry, and headed en masse for the cricket ground.

Coming down the hill towards the oval, we felt as happy as we had in a long time. Some of us even wondered if being deprived footy had done us some good. Was it possible the Fish-Men had made us better people? Was it possible we'd learned something along the way? As we streamed through the gates, colouring our faces with yellow and green zinc, we even felt a twinge of sadness that the Fish-Men—who basically we'd wanted dead for nine-tenths of their stay— were about to leave.

And that's when we saw them. They were waiting for us, in the middle of the oval, standing defiantly by the cricket pitch.

The leader bounded out to meet us as we neared the middle. We knew what his rotten flabby lips were saying, before he even hit the translate button.

But he hit the button anyway, and out came the words that were like daggers to our hearts: 'No cricket. One year. Mind experiment. On this town. No cricket,' he announced, producing a ray gun and liquidating a Gray-Nicolls bat one of our men was holding. Then, turning the gun on us, he added:

'Understand?'

[First published in *Tincture Journal*]

Vanessa Craven

Vanessa lives in Daylesford, having made the 'tree change' from Melbourne.

She hails from the foothills of the Himalayas in India.

She is a Librarian as well as a singer songwriter.

She enjoys writing short stories and poems with the Moorabool Writers Group, and 'Off the Cuff' Poetry Group.

Starting A Fire Without Matches

High in the foothills of the Himalayas, 6000 feet above sea level, in Mussoorie, stood my Nana's four bedroom, solid stone, whitewashed house, with its green galvanised tin roof. The house overlooked the centrepiece –*'her garden'*.

It was a crisp autumn morning. How I absolutely loved this weather! The sun was filtering through the trees into my bedroom.

I was tucked snugly in my bed, under a down quilt with a flannel sheet. The pillowcase which had some potpourri hidden in it, smelled quite nice. Nana often did this, to get rid of the musty smell that often hung around the bed clothes, after the dampness of the monsoon season.

I woke up to the sound of raucous crows, mynahs and sparrows creating a cacophony of gleeful sound. In the distance a cuckoo added its symphonic rounded notes.

In the bird bath close by, a Verditer flycatcher was enjoying itself splashing water with wild abandon, savouring every moment of its morning ritual

In the evenings, sometimes, a 'cheer' or pheasant would alight on the boughs of the tall Cedar in the middle of the garden, and call out to its mate.

If one listened really carefully at night, when the bedroom window was open, one would hear a lone owl hooting in the distance. It added a spookiness to the darkness outside.

The garden was huge. Carefully laid paths wove intricately and enticingly around the garden, beckoning one to explore what lay around the corner. A variety of flower pots, which had been recycled from 'dalda', (20 lt. margarine canisters), had been painted green and were placed strategically around the garden. Luscious plants cascaded prolifically down the sides of these transformed tins.

There were neat flowerbeds with rock walls placed around large oak, maple and coniferous trees. Beautiful native bushes and plants including exotic species, all had a specific position where they thrived without restraint. Myriads of flowers and scents pervaded this enchanted garden. It was a haven for birds, bees and bugs of many varieties.

Many a time I would walk with my Nana through this garden. She would name all the plants, and I would have to remember them all, with the correct spelling and botanical name. Thus began my early botanical education!

The garden was the apple of her eye. Many prizes were won at local flower shows. Her gladiolas, dahlias, lilies, roses, chrysanthemums, carnations, hyacinths and rhododendrons all thrived and blossomed in this cool climate, in such colourful array. Then there were the jasmine and honeysuckle creepers as well as the 'lady of the night, which was right next to my bedroom window. Hmm! Such memory jolting smells, as I think back on the days of my childhood, in the Hill-station.

What really caught my attention on this particular morning was a plume of smoke in the corner of the garden. It was thick! I could hear someone puffing, blowing and wheezing, punctuated by coughing and spluttering. There was the sound of air being blown into an old metal pipe, the sound of a badly blown flute! It had been transformed from an old bit of railing into a 'phookni' or 'blow pipe'.

I could make out the figure of Mungalee (Mung-ga-lee), the gardner who was in his late fifties. He was clothed in his blue surge jacket, crisp white pyjamas and white turban. He was shaking his head and twirling his full blown moustache as he stared at the stubborn fire. He muttered to himself and swore under his breath. He wasn't having much luck at all! He was doing what all good gardeners do in autumn, and was raking up the leaves and debris to burn them.

The recent storm had strewn branches and leaves causing much havoc and disarray. The cold frost and recent rainfall had dampened this raw material, adding further to his woes. Poor old Mungalee, was having a 'devil of a job' starting up the fire.

I raced outdoors, like an eager puppy and greeted Mungalee. He was happy that I had emerged on the scene. Here was someone he could confide in. I was eight years old and always had fun helping him tidy up and rake leaves. Sometimes my over- zealous assistance was more of a hindrance and on such occasions, Mungalee would click his tongue and say, 'Missy Baba! Nahi! Nahi! Aisa, nahi! Aisa nahi!' in Hindi. (which meant 'Young girl!' ' No!' ' No!' ' Not like this!' 'Not like this!').

On this particular morning, my eight year old brain was in overdrive. I had observed 'Kester', who was a boarder at Nana's Place, do what I was about to do.

I told Mungalee I had a great idea of how to get his fire started. Before he could ask what I had in mind, I raced back into the house, and rushed back with a tin of powder. Without further ado, I sprinkled it generously upon the smoking fire.

Mungalee had his face close to the ground, blowing at a beleaguered dying flame buried in the midst of this mass of debris and leaves.

Suddenly there was a hiss, accompanied by several pops and a huge BANG! The flames shot up, and so did Mungalee! He yelled 'Hai! Hai! Khuda. O my God! O my God!' He roared with fright and pain and coughed, as though he were having a seizure!

His face was blackened, and suddenly looked terribly lopsided! More than half of his pristine manicured moustache and bushy eyebrows were missing. More so down the right side of his face, which was closest to the pile of debris.

I leapt back, as much from the explosion, and rising flames, as from a roaring Mungalee! I had never seen his pallor so 'darkened with rage'. Most of his highly prized and prolific moustache was gone! Reduced to ashes! There was not much left to twirl and commune with, when big decisions were being made in the garden! How could he face his wife and family and his peers with such a shocking change in his appearance? A man without his 'full blown moustache', was like a dog without its bone!

I apologised profusely. Promising Mungalee that his moustache would soon grow, and that after all – my Dad's gun powder had helped start the fire. Some good had come out of this well- meaning exercise!

Mungalee wasn't to be consoled by any of this patter, and told me in no uncertain terms that he would tell the 'Sahib' (my father), what had happened.

Dad was very careful with his guns and related paraphernalia, however this time the gun powder had found another use.

I dreaded the tanning that I would undoubtedly get!

The time for reckoning was drawing near!

Mother's Day

Mother's Day this year 2016,

Without you, was so strange!

I yearned for your smile,

Your nod of approval,

Instead, I went to your graveside,

Placed your favourite flowers,

Warm colours of yellow and purple that you liked,

No cake and sandwiches or a cup of coffee,

As we used to do, to celebrate.

No presents to open,

No photographs to remember the event,

Just a headstone,

A windy graveyard,

And pouring rain!

I felt the pain.

My 'Mop Top' Tree

You were a tiny sapling when I bought you.

Little did I know, then,

How prolific you would be.

Your girth grew, your branches too, with thick lush foliage,

Stopping the sun getting through.

Those hot sunny days, definitely much cooler,

Sitting under your gaze.

Nestling in your branches, birds safely hidden from sight,

But for the sound of their chirping and twitter,

O, and all the 'bird crap' on my outdoor table and chairs,

I hastily scrub off, time and again,

Before friends arrive, for a glass or two and a natter.

Sitting beneath you, my prized shady tree,

I wouldn't change you, for anything.

I thought I'd lost you, when the freak storm hit,

Tearing off one of your beautiful branches.

Your limbs laid bare and gaping,

The ants crawling all over, savouring your sap.

A 'yellow ribbon' now holds you together,

You've done well to survive all sorts of weather,

Not to mention, that rigorous pruning,

To help lighten your weighty arms.

Yet, each spring, you spring back to life,

Defying the odds, with an abundance of grand, green foliage,

That just grows bigger and wider than ever before.

As each year passes, I am thankful you are still around.

Regaining your rounded 'mop toppy', top heavy shape,

Standing firm, and shapely, my beloved 'Mop Top Tree'.

Tim Hogan

Tim Hogan has lived in Bacchus Marsh for 21 years but grew up on the flat dusty plains of the Riverina. Before finding his niche as a librarian he had stints as a labourer, cleaner, car park attendant, postie and a clerk. He has long been fascinated by the bizarre life of Andrew George Scott, priest turned bushranger.w

Court Day, Bacchus Marsh, 2015

Friday morning clusters of people
mill about in front of the stone-faced
palace of justice:

Young men hunched, smoking nervously,
discomfited by ill-fitting cheap suits and ties,
shirt tails partly exposed,

Wait anxiously to enter the solemn edifice,
hoping for leniency, for three months' suspended sentence,
for affray and disorderly conduct.

'Thank you, your Honour,'
and they'll be on their way.

Older men in smartly-fitting suits,
with briefcases, and no shirt tails exposed,
pace impatiently.

Planning appeals soon to be approved or rejected.
Jobs and money on the line. Time is money,
and lawyer's time moves more slowly than most.

Young women with children in prams and on their hips.
How tired they look, how fearful they seem.
Grandmas in support, giving loving cuddles,

hoping the magistrate will extend restraining orders
to keep violent partners away.

Saturday morning: all clear, all quiet.
The stone courthouse, survivor from gold rush days,
beckons the passer-by to inspect its imposing walls

and rest under its shady verandah,
to read the historical information marker
and imagine the course of justice in an age

when floggings, hangings, and the shooting
of rebel miners
was the daily business of this court.

In Need Of Moral Guidance

1868, the Reverend Andrew George Scott,
a.k.a Captain Moonlite,
arrives in Bacchus Marsh

Bacchus Marsh 1868

'You could be forgiven, Mr. Crook, for thinking me quite mad. Indeed, I have been judged so many times. I will try and tell you why, although such perceptions are unfounded and are careless errors of judgment.'

The speaker of this startling statement was the Reverend Andrew Scott, newly appointed as an assistant minister at the Holy Trinity Church, Bacchus Marsh. He was addressing James Elijah Crook, a prominent man of local commerce and industry and a leading member of the Holy Trinity congregation.

'It is an amalgam of several factors,' continued the Reverend Scott. 'Firstly, there is my general countenance. In company before I have even spoken it may be observed that I linger in my gaze at people and objects for longer than polite society would expect. My mind, my eye, is readily fascinated by my surroundings, distracting me from civil intercourse with people in my company. In the initial instance perhaps it is judged as rudeness, over a period perhaps as a touch of lunacy.'

The large and rotund figure of James Elijah Crook was sitting in his chair sipping gently on some brandy as the Reverend Scott gave this explanation. At the mention of the word 'lunacy' his eyes lifted a little from his glass and fixed on the Reverend Scott for a moment, but a nod of his head and another sip of the brandy enjoined his guest to continue his monologue. A conventional man he was but one with a natural curiosity about the world and the people he met so he had not yet formed the view that the Reverend was mad.

The Reverend needed little encouragement to continue.

'While I gaze at length at many things around me my mind is galloping with a thousand thoughts. Each of these I welcome, though naturally they at times overwhelm me. They collide in my consciousness, shattering into more thoughts as a swirl of fragments which both dazzle and obstruct me.'

The Reverend could see that his free-ranging exploration of the inner workings of his mind and consciousness had taken Mr. Crook a little aback. He had noticed a slight recoil in his posture and a quizzical look creasing across his face; signs that the conversation was drawing his host into some uncomfortable territory.

'But one must be open to such a sensory revelation, sir' he reassured Mr. Crook. 'It is all part of how the Lord reveals his creation to us.'

'Reverend Scott, I hope you will pardon me saying this but I fear that this bombardment upon your senses may disrupt you from your spiritual work and obligations.'

'On the contrary, sir. Such a bombardment, as you describe it, is to be embraced. Did not God create us with a sophisticated sensory capacity and a mind sufficient to process and filter all of his creation? To close oneself to this would be to censor, or even deny, what God himself has put before us.'

Mr. Crook grasped his brandy a little more intensely but otherwise gave the appearance of calm reflection on this discourse. He was about to respond when the Reverend's attention was drawn to a young man who entered the room. He was of medium height, around five foot and eight inches with a slender frame. He was smartly dressed in a short frock coat with a check waistcoat. As Scott's gaze rose above James Crook's face he turned to see who it was.

'Ah, it is you, Robert. Let me introduce you to our visitor. This is the Reverend Scott, recently arrived in the Marsh to minister at Holy Trinity. Reverend, my eldest son, Robert.'

Reverend Scott rose sharply to his feet and offered his hand in greeting. He noted at once Robert's soft and elegant hand.

'How very good to meet you, Robert.'

'Indeed, Reverend, I am pleased to make your acquaintance. There is much talk in the town of your first sermon, I am sorry I missed it.'

'Yes, I understand so. Your father and I have been discussing this among other matters.'

The Reverend was a little slow to release his grip from the handshake taking just a moment to form a first impression of the young man's countenance. This was a habit of his when he was introduced to men and women alike. He believed the initial sensation of someone at the moment of introduction was often a revelatory moment where a glimpse of a person's true spirit was briefly revealed. This was a moment to be seized upon to gain some insights, which would not be possible later when the formality of good manners and people's natural inclination to be wary of strangers hid some of their emotions. The young Crook made two immediate impressions upon the Reverend. One was that of a young soul with a deep but unrecognised yearning for something. The other was a perception of someone with a gentle but clearly discernible sense of his own nobility. That such profound insights could be formed in a moment the Reverend had no doubt. It was a skill that could be harnessed if one was fully open to receiving all stimuli that one was exposed to, as he had earlier been telling Mr. Crook.

'Father, I do wish to speak to you. It is a matter of some import.'

James Crook's nose and cheeks wriggled a little at this request and he let out a frustrated sigh.

'Please, Robert, it must wait awhile. I have some matters I wish to discuss with the Reverend and I do not wish to detain him for longer than necessary'.

'Father, please, I have been trying to speak to you for some time.'

'Mr. Crook, please, do not preference my time above your son, it seems the boy has good cause to speak to you urgently.'

'Now, Reverend, let me be the judge of what is urgent and what is not. Do not the scriptures tell children they must obey their parents?'

'Indeed, sir, they do and if I am not mistaken the verse you refer to also warns fathers not to exasperate their children!'

Robert Crook flashed a grin at this rejoinder but his father screwed his eyes together and gave a dejected shrug of his shoulders. He was a man knowledgeable of his Bible but the Reverend Scott's reputation as an orator and intellect had preceded his arrival in the town. He now saw why.

'Very well. For the sake of familial harmony, Robert, I will speak with you directly after I have spoken with the Reverend. It will be no more than another five minutes. I give that as a promise in front of the Reverend who I am sure will hold me to account.'

'Yes, Father, since you have promised so in front of the Reverend, I will wait for you in the back parlour.'

On Robert's leaving of the room the two men then returned to their conversation. While James Crook maintained some curiosity about the Reverend's theories of psychological phenomena his real purpose in inviting the Reverend to his house had been to discuss with him some matters more practical. For some time the town had been in a state of alarm over an increase in petty thieving and acts of vandalism. The suspected culprits were thought to be local youths but unfortunately the constabulary had only apprehended a few of the perpetrators. As a leading citizen of the town James Crook had formed a view that some moral instruction to the community would be helpful in reducing the incidences of these crimes. Who better to deliver this message than the young and vigorous Reverend Scott, a decorated veteran of the Maori wars in New Zealand, no less, before answering God's call to the priesthood.

'Reverend Scott, your theories of psychological phenomena are indeed arousing and I am not at all hostile to them. I do however have something of a more practical nature to raise with you. It concerns the youth of this town and their need for some moral uplifting.'

The Reverend Scott leaned in towards James Crook placing his two hands together as if about to begin a prayer and said, 'Mr. Crook, I am at yours and the town's service. If there is a problem concerning the youth of this town then you will find me most vigilant in providing the youth with some moral guidance.'

Mr. Crook looked well satisfied with this transaction in the manner he might when concluding one of his profitable commercial agreements 'You have my gratitude, sir. I shall not detain you any longer,' and then, pausing for a moment and tapping his finger to his cheek, said, 'lest I should 'exasperate' my son, eh?'

The Reverend then took his leave, politely refusing any accompaniment to the door. He had much work to do and he resolved to set all his mental and emotional faculties to the task he had been set. In his mind the object appeared to be to provide some digestible moral inspiration through an emotional connection with the wayward youthful souls of this community. The prospect of this activity energised him as strode back to his lodgings, his frock coat flapping as he mind swirled with ideas.

Shirleyrose Rowe

Bacchus Marsh resident for 33 years. As 'Shirley Smith' she was Secretary of the Chamber of Commerce and the Apple Valley Festival. Private pilot of single and twin engine light aircraft. Self-published 'Rose Cottage Bacchus Marsh'. Changed name to Shirleyrose Rowe in 2001

The Irony Of Life

'Good morning, Shirleyrose, so pleased to meet you. I am Stephanie Blair, reporter for The Local Newspaper.'

'Hello Stephanie, I have ordered coffee is that okay?'

'Sure thing. This is a charming old fashioned sort of cafe.'

'Mmm it is my favourite, and thank you for asking to interview me in relation to the book I have just self-published. It is not easy to promote it myself – not at my age anyway. I haven't the same network I had when I was in the aviation industry.'

'Oh, and where did you work?'

'Well, I was a pilot first, flying light aircraft. Then I worked at Moorabbin Airport at three different businesses over the years.'

'How fascinating to meet a woman pilot. I am really interested in writing an article on your outlook on life as your book gave me tantalising insights to a very strong, courageous woman. So perhaps for my readers you could describe yourself. A slightly different approach which I like to achieve.'

'That is different! Well, I am 74 years young at this time, and yet I am told I look younger.'

'Goodness, I couldn't agree more. Sorry! Go on.'

'160 centimetres tall, with a small oval face, straight nose fair skin and sparkling eyes that change colour according to the clothes I wear, combined with a short stylish cut of white hair. Oh yes. I forgot to include the glasses, which look attractive but I wish I could see clearly without them. A cheeky grin, bright personality and a caring nature about sums me up.

During the Depression, my mother looked after her father who was ill with Tuberculosis. Depriving herself of food to feed her family, she became infected. At this time arrangements were made for her to go to the Greenvale Sanatorium which meant that decisions had to be made about the rest of the family.

My mother asked that her two babies be brought up together as we had been looked after by relatives until then, and it was her dying wish. At my present age, Nana accepted the role of mother to her two and five year old grandchildren.'

'Was your Nana on your mother or father's side of the family, Shirleyrose?'

'She was Dad's Mum, Stephanie, and though quite strict, my brother and I felt loved. I was aware that I was different to my friends because they had a mother, not a grandmother.

I can clearly remember after being admonished for some naughtiness, giving my dog a hug while telling him, "I know you love me and when I grow up and have children, if God will let me look after them until they are old enough to look after themselves, I won't mind dying."

I've never had any fear of dying. I was a serious child, and we had lots of chores to do to help Nana, and we made our own fun.

In 1940 when I was a teenager, my father married again. It was one of those wicked stepmother situations that leave children bewildered.

I fell in love with a Rover Scout at age 15, who later became a bell-bottom sailor whom I loved dearly. I rejected advances from at least two nice boys because 'he' was overseas on duty. This was being a teenager when you could not be – not the same as pre-war anyway.

I absolutely loved ballroom dancing, which I had to learn by 'following my partner' as I couldn't afford dancing lessons. Sewing, cooking and bike riding I enjoyed and I worked in an office.

At age 17, I had my driver's licence and Dad bought me an old A Model Ford car – worth $25,000 on today's market. It was sold to buy a block of land when the sailor and I married in 1948.

Are you sure you are interested in all this reminiscing Stephanie? Surely your readers would not be interested?'

'Just let me be the judge of that, Shirleyrose, remember I am the reporter!'

'There isn't really a happy ending you know! We were happy in those days. Dad and my brother and his wife helped us build our weatherboard home. Our first daughter was born and she didn't eat and sleep as I expected babies did, so that was a shock to the system!

Our son was next, and on the day he was born, I thought I had stomach pains from something I had eaten! Another two loved daughters, but by then business commitments overshadowed family ones. The 'home maker' and the 'provider' seemed to travel ever diverging paths at this time, but I would have staked my life on our love. I worked hard to combine mother and lover roles to the best of my ability.

Then, everything fell apart. I became jealous of my best friend – with justification as it turned out. I even learned to fly aeroplanes on the basis of, if you can't beat 'em, join 'em, and I succeeded very well – twin engines and all, but it didn't help me to keep my husband.

History repeated itself with my other best friend, so with disillusionment came divorce.

Many years later, I am bright and bubbly again, and no longer a door-mat. Fit and healthy, always busy and usually helping others.

The irony of life is that my ex-husband (two wives later) wants me to live the rest of our lives together on one of the Solomon Islands!

THANKS, BUT NO THANKS!'

Light At The End Of The Tunnel

The little girl paused with the scissors in her hand ready to cut another chunk out of her shiny straight blonde hair.

'Rosie, where are you? Your mother wants to see you now!' called her father as he walked down the hallway.

Rosie was hiding under her bed and deliberately cut some more hair. Strange things were happening, things she didn't understand. No one was paying her any attention. Until now they had not noticed that she wasn't playing in the sand pit where she was supposed to be.

'Rosie! Rosie! Are you playing hidey, come on, little Princess? Come out, come out wherever you are?'

Muttering to himself, her father walked into the bedroom saying, 'Well Jess, I can't find her. She's not in the sand pit or outside in the yard so she must be in the house somewhere.' Jess was sitting up in bed, looking tired but happy. Beside the double bed a small washing basket held their new born baby boy.

'With all the hustle and bustle over the past few hours, I don't suppose you've paid her much attention love,' Jess replied.

'Yes I have!' he retorted defensively. 'I read her stories and played with her, but since the baby was born I guess I lost track of time. I thought I should help the midwife tidy up and she has only just left.'

Just then a plaintive voice called out, 'Daddy, I'm hungry.'

Bill bounded out of the bedroom to see their little daughter standing in the kitchen doorway, and his jaw dropped. She was wearing a soft cotton dress with rosebuds embroidered around the hem, and one pantie leg showing beneath the hem and her hair was all 'skew-whiff', sticking out at all odd angles.

'Rosie,' he cried, 'what's happened to your hair?'

As he reached out to hold her, Rosie's large blue eyes filled with tears.

'I cut it to look pretty, don't you like it, Daddy?'

Bill held her close, stroking the child's head, saying, 'Little Princess, it looked pretty the way it was, didn't you know that?'

His thoughts were in turmoil. Had she cut her hair because of the new baby? Surely that couldn't have anything to do with it. How to understand a three year old?

One good thing about not having much work was that he could be at the birth of his second child, which was a miracle in itself. He shook his head, realising that daydreaming wouldn't help telling Rosie about her new baby brother. Right now, she was more interested in food.

'Rosie, we've been very busy for a while because Mummy has found a little baby boy to be your brother. He's asleep now, but I was trying to find you so that you could cuddle him. Would you like that?'

Rosie's head gave a little nod.

Carrying her into the bedroom, he put her down beside the basket. Her gaze wandered from the baby to her mother and back again. Jess, having heard Bill's exclamation over Rosie's hair, hid her shock and disappointment. She smiled at Rosie, 'Little Princess, your baby brother's name is 'Billy', and when he gets bigger he will be able to play with you. Won't that be good?'

Again, Rosie's head gave a little nod. Leaning over the basket, she kissed the baby's forehead and smiled. Bill and Jess smiled at each other. Aged 27 and 22 years of age respectively, they were still very much in love.

Perhaps the very fact that times were hard and they tried to live a day at a time bonded them more closely. They had their 'pigeon pair' now and Rosie's hair would soon grow.

However, no one knows what the future holds, what possibilities and challenges we must address during our lifetime. The light at the end of the tunnel always beckons.

Rose Cottage Bacchus Marsh

History of an Era with Recipes 1888 – 2002

Extract from my self- published book

'Greystones' is a property which extends along Rowsley Valley and part of the Brisbane Ranges at Bacchus Marsh. Many years ago it extended much further towards Geelong as part of the Glenmore Estate.

Located on the property is a two storied bluestone, Gothic style homestead, which was designed by architects Taylor & Wyatt and built by G. Kirby, in 1875-76, for Molesworth Greene.

The property had a network of buildings, including a substantial stable, workshops and houses which formed an almost self-contained complex.

Molesworth Greene earned respect, as under his guidance 'Greystones' was a leader in agriculture and animal husbandry.

Miss Greene, who never married, was intensely interested in the 15 acres of the garden. The eldest daughter of the gentry was always addressed and referred to as a 'Miss' while subsequent daughters were addressed by their Christian names.

Henry Burbidge was employed as Head Gardener at 'Greystones'. Rose Larkin was employed as a parlourmaid. Rose reveled in working amongst the fine furniture, exquisite china and crystal in the beautiful oak paneled country mansion. She was often heard to remark, 'I would rather have one Irish linen tablecloth than six cotton ones.'

Like a fairy tale, the gardener and the parlourmaid fell in love.

Prior to their wedding, Henry bought a double block of land in Gell Street, Bacchus Marsh. One block was to be a flower and vegetable garden and their home was to be built on the other. The two room weatherboard cottage Henry built for his 'bride to be' was called 'Rose Cottage' in her honour.

Rose and Henry were married at Clifton Hill on 25 January 1888.

During the 19th and early 20th centuries, it was general practice for families to possess a family Bible. This was also used to record births, marriages and deaths of the family. A Bible was usually given to a child at some stage in their life with an understanding it would be used in this way.

Henry and Rose had eight children who were all born in the main bedroom and were delivered by the local doctor. As the family grew, two more rooms had to be added. The two front rooms became the parlour and the main bedroom; the additional rooms then became the dining room and another bedroom. Eventually, Rose Cottage became a six room home.

Charles Burbidge was the last child born, and his granddaughter, Helena Wayth, was 'Miss Victoria', then later 'Miss Australia' in 1991.

The two blocks of land were divided by a fence covered with rambling roses. Beside the house was a driveway of compacted dirt and white pebbles which led to a stable at the back. Housed in the stable was the horse that pulled the jinker in which Henry travelled daily to 'Greystones'. When he retired the stable became an all-purpose shed covered with roses.

'The coldest hour of the morn is the hour before dawn', was often quoted by Henry. He was always up and around from about 4.30 am to be ready for when his brother Bob called at Rose Cottage to pick him up at 6.30 am. Bob lived around the corner in Bennett Street and 'he used either a pony and jinker or light Spring Cart to travel the seven miles to 'Greystones' to start work at 7.00 am. The locals always said they could 'set their clocks' by the clip-clop of the Burbidges going past.

With such a large family, the responsibility of cooking, cleaning, washing and ironing became a heavy burden for Rose.

The eldest daughter, Elizabeth, was trained to be a 'mother's help'. As the third oldest, Lottie was given such tasks as 'running messages' and, on Saturdays, she sat outside polishing the family's shoes ready for Church on Sundays.

Monday was washing day. With no mod cons, Rose faced a fearsome task. By the time the children left for school, the sheets would be boiling in the copper. With so many girls, imagine how many dresses, petticoats and pinafores there were to be washed and later ironed. If the socks were hanging on the line when the children returned from school, they knew their mother had finished.

Tuesday was another hard day. The clothes had to be ironed with flat irons heated on top of a wood stove. On hot summer days the kitchen would be like a furnace, for the fire would be going for hours.

Frequently on a Saturday afternoon, Rose 'did the church flowers'. After all, she had a large garden upon which to draw!

The social life of Rose and her girls revolved around the Holy Trinity Church of England in Bacchus Marsh. The girls sang in the church choir, attended Sunday School, and church services, and they also belonged to the Girls' Friendly Society.

The males of the Burbidge family were less enthusiastic about church attendances. Sport was their great love.

On winter evenings, with no radio, Rose would read to her family, usually around the family room fire. Lottie claimed they must have had the whole of Dickens read to them! Yet, even Rose thought it 'unsuitable' for a small girl when Lottie won a copy of Bunyan's Pilgrim's Progress for a school prize.

Olive, Hetty and Rosie contracted typhoid fever in 1905. This epidemic lasted from March until October, affecting many other adults and children in the area.

Aged 10 years Rosie was a pretty child with a mass of golden curls and when she died of meningitis at the Children's Hospital in Carlton in 1909, her little body was sent home by rail.

Amongst the family papers was a lovely tribute to the memory of their little girl:

In memoriam

God gave me a beautiful flower

I kept it for ten long years

I nursed and tended, and loved it so,

To my soul it was very dear

So dear that I knew each changing smile

or shadow that crossed her face

I could tell each one of her locks of hair

They fell in a nameless grace.

She bloomed so fair and how it befell

I never in time shall know

But my blossom drooped and a shadow fell

Over all my life below.

Even now my heart rebels and longs

For that which cannot be

Though I know she has gone to a pleasant land

And is waiting there for me.

Nicole Smith

Nicole is a qualified writer who currently volunteers for the Gordon News.

Nicole was chatting with a woman from Gordon last year and discovered her first prize-winning poem in high school was about the woman's great, great grandfather. 'Everything comes round,' Nicole commented at the time.

From that six line piece to short stories, travel tales, cookbook (editor), even a romance novel; Nicole writes anything.

Easter

From heaven, to hell, and back again.

Bathe me in a pool of warm melted chocolate

With a rainbow of M&Ms floating around

Pop in a few pink and white (bunny) marshmallows

This is one form of heaven I've found.

Pin me to a cross with nails piercing my hands

Blood pooling, from droplets, below

See me die slowly, hanging there

And just wait 'til the moment of no more glow.

And on Sunday

I will rise again

Short and simple

It is your win.

Amen.

Little Incubation Girl

As I stand beside you

In your tiny incubator

A warmth overwhelms me

Continuously

Softness beneath me

Beneath you -

A thin, white, cleaned sheet

Your little breaths in and out

Consoling me that you are here

Still with me

Even with your yellow skin

Be gone 'in weeks' they say

My precious, tiny bundle

Lying as a tight ball

Illuminated blue

Criss-crossed hair net

Nappyless

So, so cute

Gorgeous

My truly beautiful

Precious baby

Little incubation girl.

Let's Get Dirty!

Oh yes, let's

Get very, very dirty!

It's been awhile

Almost a year

Since I got dirty

With you.

But the time is here

To dress in gloves

And boots

And grab my

Tools of trade

Get down on my knees

And attend to

Your every desire

So here I am

Cleaning the fish pond

With the little goldfish.

Confusion

When I wake
Where am I?
I don't know that lady
She seems to know me.
She speaks of people
I don't know them.
She tells of things -
Supposedly from my past.
How can I deny her points?
She happily chit-chats.
I nod my head,
Occasionally.
Then I tire.
Nodding off.
She kisses me
Gently on my forehead.
That's nice.
Waking later
There's that feeling.
Someone's been here.
Aarrrr, yes I remember!
My darling wife.
Next second...
I wonder who that could've been?
A rosy perfume lingers.

Mathew Barton

Matthew Barton has always wanted to write and only recently finished his first short story. He currently resides in Bacchus Marsh with his wife, Mikaela. He is working on his first novel.

The Magician

Prologue

I always wanted to be a magician. Ever since I was a little kid. I would practise for hours and hours with a deck of cards, or coins, or the cup and ball trick. Anything I could get my hands on. I'd forever be asking my parents to pick a card.

At the age of eleven I built up enough courage to enter the school talent contest. I was going to amaze everyone; I just knew it.

Leading up to the big day I was more nervous than I'd ever been in my life. I ramped up my practice and got my performance flawless so I couldn't possibly get anything wrong.

A few days earlier, my mum had helped me make a magician's cape—flowing and black. It was clichéd but I loved it. The night of the performance I also planned on wearing a top hat and coattails. I was going to be a real magician.

Finally the time came and I stepped on stage. I was so nervous my hands were shaking and sweaty. I took a deep breath and introduced myself . . . and felt a wet, warm stain spread down my leg.

I raced off stage and, after a lot of convincing, my parents let me change schools.

I gave up performing magic in public after that, but never gave up on my dream of one day becoming a world-famous magician.

Now, ten years later, here I am. World famous. Performed around the world. Won numerous awards. I've worked with the best: David Copperfield, Penn & Teller. You name it and I've worked with them.

The problem is, if you make a deal with the devil, one day, they're going to want you to repay your debt.

Chapter 1

'Another fantastic show, Seb!'

'Thanks, Carla,' I said. 'You were fantastic, too. I wish I knew how you could contort your body to fit into those small gaps.'

'I can always show you,' Carla winked at me. 'Again, that is.'

We were backstage after another sell out show in Los Angeles. Night five of ten—all sold out. Carla was still in her red, low cut, slimming dress and fully dolled up—her blonde hair flowing. She did exactly what she was hired for: distracting the audience. Not only that, however. She was a damn good assistant.

'Give me an hour,' I winked back at her. 'I've got autographs to sign.'

Carla gave me a quick peck on the lips and rubbed her hand against the front of my pants. 'Don't keep me waiting too long.'

'Now, Carla,' I said taking her hand. 'I can't deny the crowd what they want.'

Carla pouted, which somehow made her cuter. 'And what about me?'

'I would never forget you,' I smiled. 'Meet me at my hotel room. You still have the key?'

She made a waving motion with her hands and then plucked the keycard seemingly out of thin air. It was a trick I'd taught her.

'You're getting better.' I kissed her again. 'See you soon.'

I turned and left the room and headed back to the foyer of the venue where we were performing. Waiting for me was a massive queue of eager fans, all awaiting a signature, photo, or both and, of course, I obliged each and every one of them.

When I was finished I checked my watch and saw that over an hour had passed. I knew Carla would be impatient, but she knew this was part of the job. There were times when she joined me in the photos and signed autographs for fans as well, but tonight wasn't one of those nights. I checked my phone and, unsurprisingly, I saw two missed calls and a few texts. I quickly checked my voicemail as I walked back to the green room. They were both from Carla.

'Where are you? I'm horny.'

'I've started without you. You're missing out.'

I grinned at the thought of her lying naked on the bed waiting for me and checked my texts. Two of them were from her, essentially saying the same as the voicemails, but the other was a number I didn't recognise.

The time is now. Time for you to pay what you promised.

My mind started to race. Somehow, I knew exactly what this anonymous texter was talking about—the deal I had made six years ago.

Chapter 2

It had been another long day at school. It was the start of winter and snow was just starting to fall. I was trudging home, head down, not looking where I was going, when I bumped into something and fell onto my backside.

'Oof,' I said, as I landed painfully.

I looked up at what I'd walked into. The sun was out and was piercingly bright with glare, but it was definitely a person in front of me. He was tall and wore a large, black cloak with the hood pulled over his head.

He leant over and stuck out a gloved hand. Tentatively, I took it and was helped up. As that was happening, I got a look at his face. Two beady black eyes, thin mouth, large nose. Worst of all, however, were the scars that cut all across his face.

'You should watch where you're going,' the man said, as I dusted myself off.

'Sorry,' I mumbled and started to go around him.

A large hand landed on my shoulder. 'Wait.'

I looked up at the man. Trying not to stare at his scars, but it was hard not to.

'Your name is Sebastian, yes?'

'How-how do you know that?' I tried to shrug his hand off my shoulder, but it wouldn't budge. Perhaps he'd seen it on my backpack.

'And you want to become a magician. Am I right?'

I didn't know how this man knew these things about me, but I was officially scared. Both by what he knew and his look. No one at my new school knew I practised magic tricks. Not even my closest friends and surely I was far enough away from my old school that no one from there would have sent this man. Plus, that was four years ago.

Although, I still had nightmares about it.

'Listen, mister,' I took a few steps back and his hand dropped back to his side. 'I dunno who you are, but if you don't leave me alone I'll scream and run. So please, can I pass?'

The man continued to look at me but made no effort to move aside.

'You don't even want to know what I've got to offer you.'

So he was a salesman? That still didn't explain how he knew my name or my one and only wish.

'No, thanks,' I said, and went to walk forward, but the man didn't move. 'Let me pass please.'

The man stepped aside and I quickly walked past.

'I can help you become a world-famous magician, Sebastian!' I heard the man call after me. 'Performing magic on stage—without wetting yourself.'

I stopped. How could this man possibly know about that? I spun around, confident now this was a prank from someone I used to go to school with, but he was no longer standing there. I looked around, baffled by where the man could've gone so quickly, but there was no sign of him anywhere. I noticed something glistening on the path where he'd been standing. Slowly—as if half expecting him to leap out at any moment—I walked up to it. Lying there, in the snow, was what looked like a business card.

I bent down and picked it up.

Devon's Magic Place. The card read in shiny, gold letters. I flipped it over and on the back was an address. As much as the man had freaked me out; I was intrigued.

I looked at the card again. The address was on the other side of town. I glanced at the time on my watch and saw that my parents were expecting me home a few minutes ago. I definitely couldn't go to the magic shop tonight. The question was: when could I go?

It was a week later before I finally got the chance.

My parents had left me home alone after they decided to go to the cinema. They'd asked me along too, but I made up some excuse not to go and, no sooner were they out the door, I was on my bike.

It hadn't snowed for a couple of days, so the ground wasn't too slippery and I made good time. Once I'd arrived out the front of the building, I set my bike down and looked up at it. This couldn't be it. Surely.

It was a magic shop, like the card said, but it was old and rundown. The sign out the front was missing half of its letters and now read: on's Mag c P ace.

I pulled the card out of my back pocket and double checked the address, and, sure enough, it was right. The place didn't look open. Actually, it didn't look like it had been open in ten years. The window was boarded up and the door was covered in dust from the inside. I walked over and tried to peer in but couldn't see anything other than blackness.

Tentatively, I tried the door and, surprisingly, it opened. Inside, the dust was thick and I couldn't help but cough.

'Hello?' I called out and took another step forward. I kept the door open with my foot so I could see.

I could just make out, with the light now coming into the room, that the store was filled with magic tricks. All my favourites and more. I looked around amazed because, despite the dust in the air, all the magic tricks looked in pristine condition. A prop guillotine, a table to cut an assistant in half, even a giant saw for a magician to split themselves in half against one wall.

I didn't want to close the door for fear I would lose the light, but I desperately wanted to explore the room. Before I could decide what to do I heard a voice, making me jump.

'Someone will think we're open if you stay there.'

It was the man from last week. The one who'd dropped the card. I knew it. I let the door close behind me and the light inside subsided enough that I could barely see anything anymore.

'Thank you,' the man said. I still couldn't make out where he was. 'You found the card I left for you?'

'Ye-yes. How did you disappear like that?'

There was a flicker of light and suddenly the man was standing a few feet in front of me, holding an old style lantern. I jumped again and took a cautious step backwards.

'That's not what you want to know. Is it, Sebastian? You want to know how you can do it, too?'

I nodded. 'Yes.'

'What would you give to be a world-famous magician, Sebastian? One that doesn't wet themselves on stage?'

'Anything,' I whispered quickly.

An eerie smile spread across the man's thin lips. 'Excellent. I can help you then.'

'How?'

'A simple promise.'

'A promise?'

The man nodded. 'A promise. When the time comes, I will take something from you-'

'What?' I interrupted.

'That's not important. When the time comes I will take what is owed to me and in return, you will be famous.'

Was this guy for real? There was no way he was telling the truth. How could he help me? Even so, even if there was the most remote chance he could help I had to go for it. So I agreed.

'Excellent,' the man said and his lantern went out, leaving me alone in the dark. The man had, yet again, disappeared on me.

I rode home in a sense of shock. Surely the man was nuts. How could he do something like that for me? Better yet, how could he know those details about me? Halfway home, however, an urge suddenly came over me. An urge I hadn't had in years. The urge to perform magic live. It was so strong that, as soon as I got home, I grabbed a deck of cards and a few other small tricks and rode to a public area. There I started to perform street magic for people.

The best part was, I didn't wet myself.

Chapter 3

I quickly found Carla's number in my phone and pressed call. It rung a few times and then went to voicemail. I tried again and got the same result. Either she was enjoying herself too much or something was wrong. And I got the feeling it wasn't the first one.

Quickly I found my driver, told him I needed to go back to my hotel, and fifteen minutes later we came to a stop. I raced out of the car and through reception to the elevators. Frantically, I pressed the up button and, after what felt like hours, an elevator opened and I jumped in.

Twenty seconds later, I hopped out at the top floor: the penthouse suite. Using my keycard, I opened the door and called out Carla's name. There was no reply. I raced straight to the bedroom.

'Carla, baby?' I said, opening the door.

Somehow, part of me knew what I was going to see. Part of me didn't want to believe it could happen.

Carla was lying on the bed, naked. Her throat had been slit and the bed and her body were covered in blood. My hands went to my mouth, as I sunk to my knees. I teared up.

'We had a deal.'

I wiped my eyes and looked up. I hadn't even noticed the man standing beside the bed. The black cloaked man with the scarred face. 'What did you do?' I whispered.

'I'm not done,' the man said. 'Remember our deal, Sebastian.' And in a flash of light, the man disappeared.

I quickly raced over to Carla and stroked her beautiful face. Tears flowing freely now. After a few minutes I called the police and, two days later, was arrested for her murder. Despite my pleas of innocence, the evidence was overwhelming. My fingerprints on her body and a knife found under the bed, also with my fingerprints. I'd been set up, but there was nothing I could do. No one believed me. It was an open and shut case and I was sentenced to forty years. Even my best magic tricks couldn't get me out of this one.

Epilogue

Four years later I was sitting in my cell. Like I had many times since getting here, I was contemplating how my life had gotten to this. How I could have been so stupid? That was when I heard a movement in my cell.

'Was it worth it?' the scarred man asked me.

Margaret Healey

Margaret is a member of the 'Off the Cuff' poetry group and lives in Ballan.

Report of the Minister of
Science to the Cabinet

After Newton, we attained true grace,

And began to apprehend the grand design.

Serenity of law became us so,

We were content to wear black hats,

And sip at sober justice

While the world imbibed its wine.

But here was law and rule which none could flee

God's Bull to all, sustained with gravity.

Force came of action, Newton had decreed.

Speed weighted, force massed, the moment seized –

The world went round, so round the world we went

And here and there dropped off a resident.

We imported thus an entropy of mind,

Causing force of reason to submerge.

Some little Jew or other was it not?

Who strung together beads of mass

And bent the light of stars, then,

Behind our backs, rewired the universe.

Relatively powerless, he empowered men with birth.

Drops of blood, he reasoned, could energise the earth.

Still such a promise generated lust,

Pure light showed dimly through atomic dust.

And now god is again an Englishman.

And so convenient, parked there by the door!

The cosmos will be tethered on a string.

In this the population may believe,

Even bodies broken by dissent within,

May invent universes by the score.

This disembodied mind can be no threat,

A ghost can ever witness parliament.

Bring out your clocks, unbind their springs

Insert in each a plastic mobius strip.

We'll make the quantum leap from hand to hand!

Think of all the surplus rubber bands.

Journey Of The Midwives

A cold coming we had of it.

At the very worst time of year.

The days dry as a widow and all the green gone.

At night the dust froze

And we could see the priests whisper.

We were footsore, weary,

And regretted

The warm spring when the eyes of love

Were wakened by the new wine,

While the wedding season crossed over the land too quickly,

Catching us unaware

Bruising Shepherd's Purse and Tansy and hunting for Mother-of-Rye

Snatching sleep when we could,

Before the voices of folly were heard sobbing under the window.

Summer brought us brides again.

Ripe as peaches

Buying dowries of lambs blood and vellum at the back of the
temple door.

While the wells dried and the wine turned

And the fruit withered on the vine.

When the sand blew from the desert and scourged our skin,

And the nights howled,

We drew the dead from the dead.

Knowing how often birth and death are one.

In the Autumn lull we planted Ragwort, Groundsel and Rue

And waited for Spring, winding swaddling bands.

Avoiding the priests and tending their daughters,

Marking their days,

Finding sweet weed among the rocks, drying Thyme,

While we watched troops march along the bleached horizon.

Then in the season of dry cows, and the slaughter of kids,

When the pale sun hangs low in the dying year

The night came, fractured by a throbbing star.

We picked our way over broken rock

And found the way barred.

We who testified to Pharaoh, were shut out.

We, from whom nothing is hidden, were hidden from the child.

(At least that old fool will not bother her again:

With his pious words, his priest's kiss and his eunuch's passion)

But we fretted for the things not done:

For the blood not staunched, for the breast not offered

For the fate not chosen, for the things not seen to.

All this was long ago

And we departed that place

Travelling by night

In fear of the patriarch.

Margaret Scarff

A retired Library and Information Manager, Margaret loves reading and writing and being part of Moorabool Writers' Craft. Cat Custody is a true story containing lots of confessions about the extent Margaret went to in order to adopt a pet against her husband's wishes. Monty, a ginger cat and the reason for the custody battle, isn't innocent in all this either! He had options but chose to leave home. The serious side of Margaret is currently focused on research into the little known condition called restless legs syndrome—a condition which tortured her late husband throughout his whole life. The research process would be a lonely activity, easily derailed, except for support and advice from the Writers' Craft group.

Cat Custody

The death of a pet is a sad time with many owners wanting a replacement to help overcome the loss. But my husband Phil was adamant there would be no more pets. 'They are a nuisance at our age,' he said, and for the next few years I pined for a replacement, cajoling and begging for permission to give a needy pet a loving home. I had all but given up when a custody battle that spanned some six months took place.

Monty (not his real name)—a ginger moggy—fended for himself from a kitten. He lived outside, caught his own food, survived a savage dog attack, and got the odd pat and flea treatment from a neighbour who felt sorry for him. The owner wasn't intentionally cruel to him. The problem, as I saw it, was that he believed Monty should do what cats do well and keep his property free of mice, rats and snakes. During a casual conversation about Monty's future, his previous owner said, 'The cat doesn't mean anything to me. He's just a cat.' Monty was mangy, thin and depressed.

My story of the tug of war over Monty's custody started about four years back.

Relaxing in the lounge room one afternoon, Phil and I noticed a ginger cat staring at us through the window. I never really liked ginger cats but at this stage, if there was a glimmer of hope for me to get a cat, I didn't give a rat's backside what colour it was.

'Hello Monty,' exclaimed Phil.

Snatching at the fragile thread of hope of getting a cat, I asked the obvious, 'Why Monty?'

'I had a ginger cat in England,' Phil said, 'and when we migrated to Australia at short notice we had to leave him behind.' Phil was obviously moved, recalling the memory of his cat, and he went on to tell me that Monty was his favourite pet in England and that it had fretted and died when left behind, even though a neighbour cared for him.

My luck was in. I heard what Phil said and I felt for his loss, but this was now about my potential gain and if I played my cards right—not looking too interested in the cat at our window, holding back the flutters of excitement in my stomach a replacement pet would be found. I kept my cool and showed limited interest. By chance I had some organic chicken-breast in the fridge so I cut off a small piece and gave it to Monty. He demolished this and looked through the open door to see if it was worth a try to come inside. And so he did, and he never left. But now back to the custody battle.

A few days after Monty visited our house his owner stopped me in the street and asked if I had seen a ginger cat with a white tipped tail. Holy hell! What was I going to say? I had seen one further down the street that matched this description but... I had won Phil over and Monty was settling in quite well, but becoming the meat in the sandwich between Monty's owner and my husband was not going to be easy. And anyway, the other cat down the street could have been the one he was looking for. It was ginger and had a white tipped tail too, and somehow this helped me feel okay about what I was doing. I needed a revised strategy, and Phil being the true English gentleman he was—never taking what doesn't belong to him—was going to need careful handling. To the question put to me about a missing cat I responded 'No' in a quiet voice with an upward inflection.

Now, like Phil, I believe myself to be an honest and upstanding member of the community, but this was my dream about to come true. There was the potential here for me to get the owner's blessing and Phil's permission. But the battle that ensued—fueled with not lies, but not totally accurate responses on my part—eventually got Phil to play 'the game'. Once he told the owners that he hadn't seen the cat when it could be seen sleeping on a chair inside. Not fooling Monty's owner for one minute, he waited until he saw Monty in our garden, picked him up and carried him home to a locked garage where he would stay for a week to learn his lesson. It is common knowledge that keeping a cat inside after moving house settles it into its new environment. This wasn't a new environment, however, and so it wasn't any surprise that, once let out, Monty soon returned to our house and there he stayed until the next time his owner tried the same discipline. The mice population was probably getting out of hand at his old home and he was needed. But Monty was dining on organic chicken, served with love.

I grieved for Monty while he was locked in the garage. I wasn't sure what his owner had done with him, so, with binoculars in hand, I resorted to scanning his property (an acre roughly), but with no luck, all the while wondering what the neighbours would think of me snooping in someone else's backyard. My good friend and neighbour on the other side added to my pain. While walking past Monty's house one day, I shared the deep grief I felt for the cat I had bonded with.

Her response was, 'Well get over it. He's not your cat. You stole him.'

I needed to find someone who would understand my pain and who would help me hatch a plan. My moral compass was out of whack, I knew that. But I also knew someone who would give me guidance without altogether squashing what I was doing. I emailed my 'mad cat-lady' friend of some thirty years and got all the sympathy and understanding I was due.

So, now I had my best friend and my husband involved in a cat custody battle!

During his transition to living permanently with us, the ginger cat with a white tipped tail was renamed 'Monty'. He didn't seem to notice the name difference, and anyway, by this time he had bonded with us. His focus was on food, warmth in front of the heater, and lots of love. He also slept on our bed.

This is the end of the story about Monty so far as his determination to relocate, and my determination to help him achieve this goes. Monty's relocation was meant to be. My husband died about six months after Monty's arrival and he was there for me no matter what time of the day or night, or the weather! Monty is my companion—he welcomes me home when I return from the shops and he understands my moods when grief unexpectedly takes over. He has a cat door in the window next to my bed and comes through this, walking across me to get to the kitchen, after which time he returns to my bed, snuggles up, and contentedly drops off to sleep. I love Monty; my need for him and my need to see him in a loving home caused me months of anxiety and involving others in a badly hatched plan. But there is a moral to this story. Cats decide where they will live!

Kathy Whye

Kathy lives in Moorabool Shire with her husband. She is an aspiring writer of historical non-fiction and is distracted by family history and academic studies. The following story is creative historical fiction.

Black Skin. Wedding Dress. Not Hers

[Warning: this story contains a racial slur that was commonly used in the 1800s. The writer included it as an authentic representation of language that would have been used casually. Let's hope we never hear it today.]

She stands quite still, catching her breath and allowing her eyes to adjust to the low light in the bedroom. She is excited and the cooler air does nothing to dampen her enthusiasm to find the only unopened package. She spies it lying in dappled shade on the rough burlap bed covering.

Her excitement had started earlier - at sparrow's fart as Alfred called it. Although god knows what a sparrow was. The farts she understood. While sparkly dew clung to yellow acacia flowers the dray had arrived piled high with all the necessities of life —horse shoes and knives, powder and cartridges, flour and sugar, pots and pans, shears and seeds, and tack for the horses. What a life saver!

These autumn days were the dag end of a hot, airless, breath sucking summer that still clung to the exhausted landscape. Alfred's vegetable garden that had started out so sprightly and luscious was a desiccated rump. They were down to the last pound of flour and sugar had run out long ago. He didn't know how to hunt, except for ineffectually shooting in the vicinity of the occasional wamboin. Bullet and animal never connected but still she loved him for that — thinking his incompetence in killing was a deficit made up by his expertise in shepherding and growing a good crop of veg.

Normally she would gather food but she was too busy looking after him and the kids. Besides it wasn't her country

- even her totem, the bilpa, didn't exist here. She didn't know the lore of Wathaurong country. No one around to teach her. But there were signs everywhere that they had been here. Obvious to her eyes, obscured to the whitefella. In her isolation she assumed that they had fallen to the same bloody doom that had been the lot of her family. Still she had Alfred's protection and that counted for a lot. In a strange way she considered him her mamambon, although her mother would have shouted that he wasn't because he was just some pagan from a heathen land. Not worthy of her. The thought of her dead gunni brought tears to her eyes.

She had turned her attention to watching quietly as he orchestrated the unloading. It was a quick process this time. They were offloading less than usual and she wondered how she could get through winter with just one bag of flour and a little salt and sugar. She was amused by his cursing when his much anticipated and endlessly described new-fangled bowie knife fell between the barrels and wriggled its way to the bottom of the load. This necessitated all the goods destined for others up the Ballaarat track to be unloaded.

She thought about her mother's tales of her family travelling light, carrying few tools and knowledge of where stores were sequestered and water could be found. Guided by songlines and stars. Now it sounded like a fantasy and she struggled to explain it. Indeed the stockmen had laughed and had told her she was a liar.

She made tea and damper for the dray master. Just before she handed him the cup he reached into the locked box under his seat and drew out a large wrapped parcel about a yard long and half of that wide. She was immediately drawn by curiosity – a delicate package, a box wrapped in a protective layer of brown, crinkly paper and tied in a cross with hairy soft baling twine. Nothing else had been packed so carefully and it piqued her attention. That and how the dray master had delicately placed it in Alfred's grimy, gnarled hands. The images jangled. Short supplies but a long winter, grubby hands holding a delicate package, the way the dray master's eyes wouldn't meet hers but eagerly reached for the tea. She struggled to make sense of it all.

Words passed between the two men. She was still learning this strange language, and when she did she would be pleased to tell you it was the fifth language she was fluent in. She caught the word 'bride' and remembered the meaning was similar to her word for buttong. Maybe she would become his buttong just as he had hinted when they started this strange journey.

Keep still she told herself. Watch. Learn the ways. Take refuge in the shadows. This was her tactic for survival. Her contemplation was broken by the noisy, tumbling, wriggly arrival of the kids – Lizzie, Lilly, George, Mary, and young Alfred up from the creek, all wet and clutching sweet shoots of cumbungi. They diverted her attention but then they always did.

She looked back to Alfred and saw him disappearing into the slab hut. The package secured firmly but gingerly between two hands. Like he didn't want to drop it and was scared he would break it. Interesting.

He was strange for the rest of the day. Normally when supplies arrived there was a buzz about the place and a generosity in his manner. The kids were given small boiled sweets and then ran around like noisy blowflies till they collapsed in a heap. There was always a treat for her too. Sometimes a new dress and once a pair of shoes. Although she wasn't sure of the worth of them.

But he was moody all day and he supervised her storing the short supplies with sharp, stabby words. She finished it all but her thoughts were on the mysterious package.

'What do you want to do with the package' she ventured.

'What package'?

'The one you put in the bedroom'.

'Nunbanna', he told her, 'nunbanna'.

She understood he was saying 'forget', in his strange way of using her words. But she thought about the bride word buttong and thought about the parcel all day.

Later, when he said he had to go see Yeomans, she immediately thought of the parcel. She imagined undoing the twine and then unwrapping that brown covering. She would have a quick look and was sure she could get it wrapped up again before he returned. She was practiced at this and while he was sharp-eyed about some things there were other things he just didn't see.

When he saddled up and rode out in the late afternoon she sent the kids to collect more cumbungi down at the creek. She wanted no witnesses. She waited for a long time under the cool verandah, until even her ears couldn't hear the rhythmic pounding of the horse's hooves. If history had anything to tell her, she knew he would be away until sundown and besides, she only needed a few minutes.

The hut was cool and the light was dim, and the bedroom at the back even cooler and darker. She stood still and let her eyes adjust to the subdued light. She couldn't believe it when she saw the package on the bed. From his manner she thought he might have locked it away in the strong box. Maybe it was for her and he had left it out for her to discover.

The twine felt soft and hairy and the knots undid easily under the expert workings of her small delicate fingers. The crackling of the paper alarmed her as she carefully smoothed down each unwrapped fold to expose the plain, brown carton inside.

It had writing on it but she couldn't read. She understood the marks meant something and conveyed messages but she only understood a few — like the mark for Whye - his mark. She saw it on the box but it was surrounded by a confusing jabble of other black marks - she knew that no matter how long she stared at it the message wouldn't talk to her.

So she lifted the top from the box, felt the soft resistance and heard the gentle sucking sound of the vacuum being breached. She thought all would be exposed, but there was another layer to get through - tied with a soft, wide, pink-silk bow. She undid it and lay the ribbon ends across the sides of the box. Now for the next layer of paper — it was white, translucent and fragile. She couldn't believe how soft it was, and how it crinkled and rustled as she gently unwrapped it. She thought that this must be the tissue paper that Mrs Yeomans had told her about - used to wrap expensive and fragile gifts.

Then the treasure was exposed. A strange, blindingly white material, neatly folded and interspersed with more tissue paper. A dress she presumed. She allowed herself the luxury of some time to trace the raised, delicate embroidery on the neckline. She had seen a similar dress when she had helped Mrs Yeomans after the birth of her first child. Mrs Yeomans said that her white dress had a special name and was only worn once. She couldn't recall the name but thought that these people had a reckless way of using resources.

She thought about the bride word she heard that morning and her heart pounded. This was true then, she and Alfred were getting married in that eccentric ceremony his people had. They would be bound for life. She hoped that was true. He was a good man this Alfred and she thought about how he had persuaded her to travel with him to Wathaurong country. It was against all lore but she knew there were new ways that came with these pale feeble people. So weak that they relied on their fearsome weapons to kill from afar and four legged yambon to carry them around. Besides she had had to escape the carnage and he had made some vague promises of a better safer life.

She gently slipped the dress from the box. Holding it gingerly by the filmy material at the shoulders she held it out from her body and allowed the dress to gently unfold. She was only 4'9' and what confused her was the length of the dress. Even as she held this shimmering loveliness at shoulder height she could see the hem folded on the dirt floor. How would she wear it? Her confusion deepened, when she saw a pair of white satin shoes separately wrapped lying at the bottom of the box. Silly Alfred, the shoes were twice the size of her feet. How would she wear them? She drew the dress against her body and held the waist in place with her forearm. She could smell the strange newness of the white linen and feel the scratchy lace. It was too long. Now how would she change that?

Her face changed from thoughtfulness to horror when she realized that there were brown smudges on the powdery whiteness of the dress. It was the imprint of her fingers.

At that moment she heard the door open.

He was furious. Shouting words she couldn't keep up with and pushing her. He snatched the dress and his face reddened when he saw how she had marked it. She tried to explain that she didn't understand that her hands would leave marks. She begged his forgiveness and tried to tell him she was sorry that she had spoilt his surprise. She loved him and Mrs Yeomans would know how to get the stains out. The dress would be ready for their wedding. Her words came out in a strange mix of Wayilwan and English as they always did when she was terrified.

He didn't understand her and his fury rose, his face apoplectic and angry. Her ears pounded with his yelled words, spit fell on her face. She couldn't understand what he was saying. She was overwhelmed. 'Slow down', she begged and reached out for his hands.

He pushed them away. 'You're just a fucking gin, we don't marry gins'. He was coarse, the words were quick and English. 'Ann'. 'New Zealand'. 'Old flame'. 'White woman'. Each word uttered with force.

The gin word echoed in her ears and strangely mixed with her agitated pulse. She couldn't think straight. She was ashamed to hear him use such language, ashamed that she had opened the package and embarrassed that she had thought that the dress was for her.

I'm leaving tonight, you pack', he shouted as he hauled the case from under the bed. Slamming it open he turned and grabbed her, pulling her roughly. 'Pack all things, not coming back. Yeomans. Here. Sundown'. Each word emphasized with a stabbing gesture.

He was giving her to Yeomans!

'Yeomans will know what to do with you and those brown brats of yours'.

She understood in that moment that she would join the station camp. She knew what that meant. 'Slow down,' she begged.

His face was a few inches from hers. He spoke slowly and loud like speaking to an idiot. She was more stupid than he thought and she couldn't even understand English.

'Black skin', he said as he jabbed her in the chest.

'Wedding dress' he bawled as he shook the dress in her face.

'NOT YOURS' – he said.

It was like a watershed. Her pulse slowed, her brain cleared. The English words came to her. She looked at him coolly.

'Five children' she said in her gentle lyrical voice, 'another on the way.'

And she thought but didn't say out loud - your loss, not mine.

GLOSSARY:

The Ngemba words are taken from a list created by R H Mathews and published in his 'Ethnological Notes on the Aboriginal Tribes of New South Wales and Victoria'. Whilst the meaning of the words are true to his listing it is not suggested that the words are accurate from an Ngemba viewpoint. They are used here to give an impression of her first language, Wayilwan, which is closely related to Ngemba.

Bilpa – Bilby, her totem

Buttong – wife

Cumbungi – bulrush

Gunni - mother

Mamambon - husband

Nunbanna - forget

Wamboin – grey kangaroo

Jem Tyley-Miller

Jem Tyley-Miller lives on a hill in Bacchus Marsh with a brewer, three free-range children and a very furry cat. She works in film and television to fund her writing obsession. Her stories have been shortlisted for the Ned Kelly S.D. Harvey Award and 'Write around the Murray. This excerpt is from her novel Afterglow.

Afterglow: Chapter 56

Leyton's Bay. Summer, 1986.

Nick's thirsty eyes devour the beachfront. Wave after sparkling wave of aquamarine meanders to the shore, covering the flat stretch of beach in a delicate, frothy lace. There is no urgency to them, nowhere else they need to be— just like all the holiday-makers who are strolling or snoozing away, or who venture into the water to play. They are exactly where Nick wants to be, but not where he is right now.

The sun bites at the back of his neck, and he wonders if these people feel it too? Just like the bites from the sand-flies who hide in his shadow. He wonders many things about these people, as he watches from behind his hunched-over shoulders, trying to disguise his coveting gaze. Mostly, he wonders what it feels to be normal. To be part of a family you didn't need to sit apart from. And what it feels like not to be embarrassed by the fact you had to hide these feelings from the people you love.

Sitting, feet in the sand, next to the grassy embankment, he makes circle-pictures with his toes while cupping his ears, trying to block out their loud Greek voices. Uncle George's voice booms as he yells across the group to his father, Gianni, and their older brother, Sifi. They are arguing about the soccer, or football as they insist upon calling it. They kick a ball around as they speak, as if it's a talking stick they need to possess before having their say.

Nick hates it when they make him join in. He wishes they'd play footy or a game of cricket instead, like the other families on the beach. The much quieter families who feel it's okay to hang out in twos or threes, or maybe fives at a pinch. Not with the entire population of a small Greek island.

The fatty lamb chops on the gas BBQ send smoke signals, alerting anyone who hasn't noticed to their invasion of the foreshore. The stench of the meat coats the inside of his nose and not even the escorting scent of lemon and herbs can cut through. He watches his Aunt Voula swatting the flies away from her face with the left over rosemary sprigs. She is deep in conversation with his mother, who is trying hard to ignore his little sister, as they lay out the salads and dips. Eleni is tapping their arms, doing cartwheels and tugging relentlessly on her mother's sleeve. She wants to be taken into the water. 'Go ask your cousin Arianna,' says his mum, as she places the spanakopita next to the olives.

Arianna is lying in the sun, the straps of her bikini pulled down so she can work on her tan. 'Can't I'm afraid, Leni. I've got my formal next Saturday and I need to look even.'

'What, even more like a hooker in your glittery dress.' Nick's cousin Fonda chimes in, as he kicks the ball back to Nick's dad.

'Skáse, Fonda! That's enough from you,' and Uncle Sifi's hand manages to twist his son's ear from where he is standing on the other side of the group.

Nick watches his older cousin poke her tongue out at her brother, before putting her head down and again becoming one with the sand.

'What about Niko? He's old enough now to look after his sister. A big nine-year-old boy.' Nick hears his uncle George pelt the ball straight back to Gianni for comment. 'He's almost old enough to start playing for Sparta.'

Nick's face burns and his nails dig into the sand, adding deep troughs to the masterpiece he's been creating.

'He'd never want to play for that team of cheats. It will be Trikala all the way. Niko, go take your sister for a swim, will you? Give us time to cook the lunch.'

His mum does not even turn from her conversation with his aunts, as she qualifies his father's request. 'But not too deep, Niko, eh? You keep her safe.'

Nick groans, hating that his cloak of invisibility has failed. Why couldn't they just have had *souvla* at home today? But the request gives him permission to get away from them. Maybe even far enough away that the others on the beach won't associate him with the loud, flavour-filled, Greek enclave. Taking Eleni's hand, he drags her off along the beach.

'Where are we going, Niko? Can I go for a swim?'

'You know you can't swim, Leni. You'll just have to paddle a bit.'

'I can too swim. See!' And she turns her arms into frantic windmills. 'I'm a good swimmer.'

'Aha.' Nick has learnt it is easier to placate rather than argue with four-and-a-half-year-old logic. 'Just stay close to me, okay?'

As they walk along the flat stretch of beach, they pass rows of coconut-smelling girls who twist and twirl their blonde hair while rubbing oil over each other's skin. They are busy feigning disinterest in the world around them—especially the world of lean, bronzed young men with wax-covered boards, who are entering the water at intervals to coast over the top of the cascading waves. Nick is amazed at their defiance of the currents that say 'you should go this way to the shore'. Up and over, they paddle out to the break where they 'sit' until a wave lets them stand and then glide on in like a wet-suited Jesus walking on water. At least that's how he decides he's going to imagine the Messiah in church from now on.

Nick looks back towards the calm waters glimmering beneath the lighthouse. He knows it would be better for him and Leni to swim there. But this would mean going past his family again. Whereas the bluff, with its jutting rocks, is far, far away. Shaped like a slumbering dragon clutching her eggs in her claws, he is lured toward her lair. He has wanted to explore her caverns since arriving over an hour ago, after watching the other dads (Aussie dads) with their sons and crab-nets combing the rocks. They had dipped in and out of the water, laughing, as they plucked what he can only imagine were the most amazing salt-encrusted treasures from the sea. 'Come on, Leni. I know a great place to swim. You see up there?'

'Up near that big, big, rock?'

'Yep, that's the one.'

'Well, come on, Niko. Let's go!' And he watches as her little legs scurry along the beach, squeals erupting as the waves wet her toes. Her dark curls bounce down her back and, as the water wets them, they hang almost to her waist. She looks back at him with her brown eyes sparkling, demanding he hurry along. His own legs, long and still not properly fitting, spring through the sand behind.

The first rock pool is shallow and wide and Leni's shrieks echo all around it, as she runs and launches into the water. Miniscule fish, the same colour as the beige sand, dart in all directions. Her tummy makes touchdown and she drags herself along with her arms. Nick steps onto the reef to watch her and stretches his arms out—like a tightrope walker—balancing his way around the edge. The dark reef here is sharp and full of holes, like the buttery cheese that Aunt Voula likes to eat, only with much more bite. Standing tall on a large, wobbling boulder, he can see enormous waves slamming down just beyond the bluff. Immediately mesmerised, he wonders if there is any way he can get a closer look.

'Come on, Leni, there's a better rock pool over here.' And he isn't wrong. Closer to the bluff they find a small stretch of beach that is part of a petite cove. The protected bay feels bespoke, created for just him and Eleni. Even the three teenage boys horsing around on the edge of a natural swimming hole—doing summersaults into the water—feel perfectly placed. As Leni makes a sandcastle full of ballrooms for her princesses and stables for their sea-horses, Nick watches the boys.

Two of them have skin almost as dark as his, tanned by the sun. But their hair is finer and sun-streaked. The other boy—a red-head—gleams whiter than the sand and is covered in patches of bright pink. His blue eyes manifest mischief as he performs for his audience. His friends egg him on, daring him to greater heights. Nick wades through the water to get as close as he can without looking obvious.

'Mate! That was a wicked double twist. Bet you can't beat that.'

'Bet you I bloody can.'

'Yeah, but this time, dumbass, don't get so close to the reef.'

'It'll all be worth it if I make it. The price for being crowned King-of-the-Reef.'

'The price for a bloody broken neck.'

Nick feels his breath suck in as the red-head takes his run up and catapults into the air. He watches his first spin, then a second and almost a third which is followed by a gut-slapping splash.

When the boys erupt into laughter, Nick breathes again. The red-head drags himself out of the water to take a bow, while the other two reluctantly applaud. 'Okay, so you officially hold the record, but just for now.'

'Come on, you two know you'll never beat that.'

'Too late for a challenge. The tide's on its way in. Besides, Tammy Whitten's bound to have pulled her top down by now. Definitely worth trying to get a look at her tits poking out from underneath.'

Nick blushes, as the boys whoop and tip toe across the serrated reef towards the beach. When they are far enough away, he wades back to check on Leni.

'Look at my castle, Niko. It's so big.' The little girl has adorned her palace with seaweed scallops, shell windows and cuttlefish walls. Two driftwood stick figures exchange pleasantries as she plays.

'That looks amazing, Leni.'

'I need to find more jewels. More princess treasure.'

'You do that then,' he says, not really listening. His eyes stare at the swimming hole where the boys had been brandishing their skills. Glancing one last time at his sister, he gathers his courage and goes over to try it for himself.

The water inside is dark green. And a curtain of olive seaweed cascades over the edges—the small, oval bubbles forming tendrils that look like alien hair. He considers the space with caution. There are more fish in here, brighter in colour. But they are still not big enough to bite. At almost four meters across, there is no opening here for shark-like things to get in. The only way in or out is over the top of the reef itself. He watches as a gentle wash of wave comes towards him and trickles down into the pond.

With a hammering in his chest, he approaches the lip. If he were to land right in the middle, he would be safe. He does the calculations in his nine-year-old mind. Three steps of run up would do. He steps backwards counting them out. One, two, three. And then, as spray from an offshore wave carries on the wind and wets his face, he runs.

Dragging himself from the water up the slimy sea wall, his arms shake from adrenaline. He feels as tall as the sun that is blinding his eyes and his muscles seem bigger than any man in his father's tough-guy films. With his grin now as wide as can be, he is on top of his world—the woes of his family forgotten. That is, until he looks for his little sister, his gorgeous Eleni, who is no longer there.

He feels his feet rip and bleed, as he runs directly towards the bluff. The dark-blue waves that were thundering out back are now just shy of the reef he is racing across. He looks down into another rock pool, heart pounding in his ears. It is empty. So he negotiates the rocky path and heads straight for the curling cliff—part of the dragon's jaw. And it is here that he finally sees her.

Squatting down, she is reaching forward into a crevasse. It looks deep, but he can't gauge the depth. He watches her wriggle, trying desperately to grab something from down in the water.

'Eleni! Stop!' But she doesn't hear him. She is too focused on what she has seen. When the wave comes crashing through the ravine, Nick watches in slow motion, as it knocks her over and she tumbles in.

Making it to the edge some thirty seconds later feels like a lifetime. And in another five he is in the swirling water too. Hungry fingers snatch at his feet from the sea grass floor, but he pushes himself upwards, grabbing her tiny body and makes for the surface.

He can swim, but not confidently in the washing machine they now find themselves in. Nestled between unyielding granite sentinels is the only way out—and anything brave enough to approach is smashing against the sides in folly. Plus it is deep. He holds the gasping Eleni as best he can and the swell tosses them from side to side. She is crying. 'Niko, help me.' But he is no longer sure that he can.

Another surge comes and both are thrust into a corner. Here, the ledge above them is high. He grabs on with one hand, but it's slippery and cuts him and they fall back into the water. He tries again, clutching the tendrils in his bloody fist. This time they hold. His frantic feet scramble, until finding a narrow ledge big enough for one foot. Standing on tippy-toe he manages to keep them secured. Leni wraps both arms around his neck, as she sobs, making him choke. Still he doesn't let go, waiting for someone—anyone—to come.

He holds Leni's slippery body with his free arm. She had passed out only moments before from exhaustion, or was it fear? He can hardly stand himself. All energy goes into holding on and keeping her mouth above the water.

But the rising tide soon covers it and he has to choose. Let go and float with her? Or hang on to the only safety he has? His cramped fist will not release and he screams as loudly as he can.

He doesn't recall which came first. The sound of someone diving into the water, or the voice that reached down and wrapped her hand around his. He remembers telling them to 'take Leni first,' then having his arm detached from his sister and being lifted up into the clouds.

When he comes to he finds himself resting under a deluge of beach towels in the shade of a bright blue tent. Looking out towards the horizon, he sees that the rock pools have all but disappeared. Only the tips of their ears poke out to warn swimmers of the sharp fangs that lie beneath in wait.

Off to the side stands a group of people who block his view of others who are kneeling. There is a stretcher on the ground. When a loud 'hup' is issued, it is raised and he sees Eleni being taken away.

Her body is covered by a blanket that looks like it's been borrowed from outer space. And a mask is covering her mouth. A uniformed man squeezes it at intervals, as he walks beside her to the ambulance that has been backed up, its lights flashing red and blue. Nick wants to cry out, to ask to go with her, but his mouth is dry and doesn't work. Instead he lies there watching as the ambulance moves off and another arrives.

His eyes loll back into his head and he takes in the red and yellow of the lifeguards, who are still standing around.

He hears their chatter: he was lucky. A bit of hyperthermia and shock, but soon he'd be right as rain. And, 'yeah, we're still looking for his parents. God knows where they've been?'

He tries hard to stay awake, desperate for news of his sister. But the voices swarm and mingle with the laughter of children still frolicking in the water and the cries of the seagulls who are arguing over nearby fish and chips. And then he hears it. Faint, but the message is loud and clear.

'They reckon the girl will make it, but her brain's probably fried. Would've been much kinder to let her drown. Still, you try telling that to the family, or to the poor little bugger here who was holding onto her for dear life.'

Nick can't hold on to anything any longer. His consciousness slips as the gurney arrives. He is followed to the ambulance by the scent of lemons, rosemary and lamb.

[Afterglow is a ghost story—a literary thriller—set on Victoria's wild surf coast. Savagely woven, it explores the death-defying bond between mother and child and questions whether or not there are times when it is okay not to let go.]

Jennie Fraine

Jennie Fraine has been involved with community writing for over thirty years. Her first collection of poetry, *The Cast Changes*, published by Abalone Press, was runner-up in the coveted FAW Anne Elder Award in 1986. Her writings have appeared in numerous anthologies and magazines.

The Decision

Sheena was eight when she decided to leave Scotland as soon as she could and forever. One afternoon, as she collected groceries from the corner shop, she met Miss McCorrie and out of her mouth popped the statement: 'I'm goin' tae Australia.'

Miss McCorrie's eyebrows rose in the middle and fell again. It would be hard to say who was more startled by the utterance. Sheena shut her mouth tight. Miss McCorrie said, 'When?' Sheena traced a circle on the counter top, around the penny she had put there. Finally, she said she didn't know, but later—when she was older—was all she knew.

Neither Sheena nor Miss McCorrie mentioned it again, though they saw each other daily at the school. Around the circumstances of her departure, Sheena wove a conspiracy of ignorance within herself. After all, it was God who engineered major steps in life like that. Sheena listened in Sunday school and did not ask questions like 'How?' and 'Why?'

Well, not often. There was that time, when the horrible Mrs McCrae, on the morning of Sheena's decision, had made an utterly loathsome statement that had turned Sheena's stomach.

'There's no good blood in those blacks or the Huns,' she had said, as if the atlas in front of her proved her point. Six years later, when the Great War began, Sheena remembered and felt sick again. But at the time she had stood up, shaking.

'You may not leave the room!'

She'd almost sat down, automatically. She straightened
again.

'Please, Miss. Surely our blood's all the same?'

Mrs McCrae's voice had come from somewhere deep in
her chest.

'Impudent child! Your father will hear about this.'

Sheena was slapped for a word out of place at home.
She may as well be slapped for two words.

'Why?' she said. And then, even more heretical: 'How
do you know what you said is true?' She expected the rotten
timbers of the little school to collapse at that instant. She felt
the air suck away from her, as the other children gasped and
lowered their heads. She felt marooned on an island of sand
which the sea was rapidly reclaiming. Soon, there would not
be a grain on which she could stand, and she would sink,
sink, sink and die. She clamped her mouth shut and sat
down heavily.

Mrs McCrae sent her out. Wordlessly. She merely
pointed her whole arm at the door. Sheena left, head down,
peeking up only to register the strange leer on Mrs McCrae's
square-jawed face. She tiptoed out of the building and then
she ran, ran all the way up the Serpentine—so-called because
it wound through the town uphill like a snake. On Sundays,
Sheena would walk along the Serpentine, feeling the calf
muscles stretch as her heels worked in their best flat shoes.
At the top, she would rest for breath. Sometimes she'd rest
halfway, look down and back over the bay towards Glasgow,
see the haze that marked its industry. She liked to think
of it as the factories' bad breath, as she watched the ferries
chugging away from the quay below her.

This day, she ran. At the top, took three deep breaths, and ran on. There were places she knew that were secluded enough to read away whole afternoons. She chose the nearest one and leaned against the yew that lived there. Would she be slapped, or caned, or belted? And when? Today was Friday, Dad would be home late and singing. On Monday he would receive the summons. So, Monday night. She had two days to live as normal. And then? Would she have to return to Mrs McCrae's stuffy classroom? Beg forgiveness? Well, she wouldnae. Never!

The force of her thoughts shocked her, for it was said in the family—and she agreed with the general view—that she was a serious and good girl. But what was the use of being serious if you couldnae stand up for what was right? And wasn't she just saying what the Minister said every Sunday: 'Love others as yourself!' Not that she loved Mrs McCrae as herself, no. She formed the Minister's own word with her mouth, but did not speak it out loud: bigotry.

Sheena spent the rest of the day on the hill, and the longer she thought about what had happened, the more strongly she felt offended. She began doodling on the ground with a twig, drawing boxes within boxes, and placed a stick figure—so tiny you could hardly see it—in the innermost one. Standing at last, she said aloud, 'The world is too sma' for us.' Who 'us' was, she had no idea. She knew no-one else who had spoken as she had to a teacher on this island.

Her mother was sewing patches on a grey blanket when Sheena returned.

'Ye're late, hin. Lard and sugar. No dawdlin' noo.'

'Aye, Ma'am.'

And until she met the lovely Miss McCorrie, she had no idea she'd made any real decisions about her future life. But Miss McCorrie was not an islander; she'd arrived two years previously to take up a post at the tiny school and, if Sheena thought 'why?' at all, it was to wonder what could have brought a beautiful young woman to this poor island?

Sheena had plenty of opportunity to entertain this thought after her scene with Mrs McCrae. Daily, she had the opportunity to study Miss McCorrie, for she was transferred to her class. In Mrs McCrae's eyes, this was a punishment bigger than the reported belting Sheena received from her father, since Miss McCorrie's students were younger and less able than her own.

For Sheena, however, the world opened up. Not only was the question 'Why?' acceptable in Miss McCorrie's classes, but Sheena was allowed to read whole days away and choose what she liked from the teacher's own small library as well. The rest of that year passed in a dream.

At the age of twelve, Sheena borrowed her brother Tom's best suit and strutted up and down Morgie Place, thumbs in braces, acting cocky. Tom was hopping mad when he found out and punched her breasts. She threw the suit out the window afterwards and stayed close to her mother. At the same time, she heard a little voice muttering in her brain: 'What does it matter? Ye'll be off to Australia soon.'

It was something she didn't know she was missing in those days: closeness. Too busy in the house with cleaning, especially around her mother's sewing machine. And outside, always the youngest child on her hip. The only chance to offload that burden came when it was her turn to bat in the summer evenings' rounders matches. Father made the balls out of rolled up paper and string. Anyone big enough to lift the bat could play.

Sheena's friends—Jeanie and Peg—were as keen as she was, and laden in the same way with their mothers' latest products. The babies were handed round, shaken if they complained. They soon learned not to.

Friends, but not closeness—Jeanie and Peg were girls to have fun with. Sheena once thought to tell them what Tom had done to her, and the pain, but found she couldn't speak of it.

They were a gang of pranksters, really. Followed each other as they matured, to make sure the boys behaved. When Willy took a fancy to Peg, Sheena and Jeanie were right behind her in the fields and hedges. Eventually, they put on Mrs McCrae's growly voice and spoke of dire punishments for bad boys.

Peg said later, 'Just as well you were there! My, how he put it on me!'

Nine in the house, boarders in summer too, and crowds at the foot of the stair in Morgie Place—it was all too much. Sheena spent Sundays on the hill reading. Skipping up the Serpentine sometimes, trudging other times. And, if anyone came past, walking demurely as a young lady should. Not exactly pretending—more like being invisible.

In her cabin, twenty-three years old and going to meet up with her man in Australia, she had a sudden insight: 'I was practising. Doing for mysel', minding my own business.' She squared her shoulders and stepped out onto the deck.

Pre-sentiment

Coyly, the clouds shroud a sky

lightening earlier, darkening late.

Sameness always turns lights on;

even the stars will blink when

the heavens again are allowed

to spread a satin lid above us.

We do not need wise men

nor glorious lowly births to bring joy

into the lives of men

who love to mow lawns and lay bricks,

or to give women's lives meaning

and an air of martyrdom.

Let the bells ring for winds

that disperse crowds, allow the light in.

Let there be frankincense and myrrh

because the earth gave us them.

Let all animal languages be heard

and translation irrelevant.

Let flocks of clouds and mass migrations

of birds be our messengers

of harmony, hope, and everlasting life

before and after us, beyond us,

among all tribes, all warring factions,

and at dawn watch all weapons turn into toys.

Amen.

On Watching The Birds In My Back Yard

There's a festive spirit out there today.

Blossoms full of nectar, grasses seeding,

and loquats dangling plump and golden.

What a feast! Families of honeyeaters

swing upside down on slim branchlets,

siphoning out sweet treats. Soldierly,

sparrows nip seeds from stalks. Less

orderly, blackbirds rummage in leaf litter.

Pigeons bob their heads as they scout for

riches fallen among stones, before taking

time out to preen, perched on wire frames.

A garden of many options. Yet even among

birds, one will send another fleeing and

come back to sing sweetly about victory.

Janelle Sheen

Janelle is the facilitator of 'Off the Cuff' poetry and 'Melbourne Communication Skills'. She is a promoter of respect and kindness along with the enhancement of communication and relationship skills specifically to reduce low-level violence.

She has been involved in education for many years, however currently is a bus driver.

Relationships

Laughter, tears
Joy and fears
Continuously flowing
Over the years

Me and you
The things we do
Arguing over
A different view

Having fun
Getting things done
Won't it be nice?
If this worked with everyone

Life's a blessing
Yet at times distressing
The import of relationships
We cannot be repressing.

Dirty Thirty

Dirty thirty

Is long in the past

Nifty fifty

Built to last

Unfortunately

Not here to stay

Even though

I'd like it that way!

Ahhh! That Was It!

Hunting high
Hunting low
Wondering where did they go

Perhaps the sea
Perhaps the snow
I really wouldn't know

Turning left
Turning right
Hunting with all my might

For what
I have forgot
Back to where it all began

Standing still
Loosen my will
Ahhh! That was it!

Hunting high
Hunting low
Where on earth did my glasses go?

Eirene Hogan

Eirene has been writing since she was a teen. A lover of history and psychology – themes that often appear in her stories - she grew up in rural Australia, spent some years trying to adapt to metropolitan city life, but finally gave up and returned to the country. She is happy now living in the Moorabool Shire, which combines the ease of rural life with the convenience of near proximity to the bustle of Melbourne. Eirene has had some pieces published on small internet websites.

Website: http://eirenehoganstories.wordpress.com/

Blog: http://eirenehogan.wordpress.com/

Email: eirene42@fastmail.com.au

Eureka

'Come on, Polly, we are running out of time. You have to put this on.' I stood in front of the unlit fireplace and held out my little sister's pinafore. The summer sun streamed in through the kitchen window and shone brightly on the linen.

'Why do I have to?' Polly grumbled as she trudged over. 'Ma didn't go to school. By my age she was a weaver.'

'That was back in the old country!' I said, as I hastily fastened her pinafore.

'I want to sew clothes, like you, Bella. I could sew beautiful gowns for all the ladies in the colony,' she said then grimaced as I braided her hair to prevent lice from making a nice cosy home in there.

Ma called out from the laundry, 'Yes, yes, Polly, when you turn twelve. That's when you shall finish school,' then she added, as she always did, 'and if you don't want to be going to school, you can start by turning the washing.' Ma spent every Monday morning in the washhouse at the back of the kitchen, turning the clothes and the linen in the big boiler, straining over the steaming water and forcing the stirrer around and around. 'Now, be off with you, your father is workin' hard at the dairy to get the money to send you to school.'

I grabbed her schoolbag and we scampered off to join our brothers. The summer heat hit us as soon as we stepped out the door, despite the early morning hour. I pulled Polly's bonnet down further to shade her eyes, but she twisted away in annoyance. 'I can do it meself.'

I could already feel the damp under my arms. I tugged at the thick linen covering my arms and envied Ned who had his sleeves rolled up to his elbows.

Ned was the eldest of the boys. He and I always took the little ones off to school, then Ned would return to join Da at the dairy and I would go off to Mrs Jones for my needlework classes, where I was learning to sew the most beautiful dresses.

We walked across the hill heading toward the marsh in the valley. It hadn't rained much over the last few years so the marsh was fairly dry. It is where the two rivers meet, the Lardedark and the Werribee, and there lies a village, our home town. Our little group wound themselves through the paddocks of Grant's land, and arrived finally at the edge of the hill. From here we could look down upon the main road; a mysterious track that came all the way from Melbourne town, went through the Marsh, then headed west into the hills and the vast unknown land full of strange trees and wild natives.

'The road is oddly quiet,' Ned said. 'Where has everyone gone?'

Usually it was full of travellers heading west. The week before we had watched a wagon full of family goods rumble past. Among the walkers a young lad looked our way, grinned and held up his pan. Today we peered at an empty road.

'Maybe Jim has found all the gold, so there is no more,' Ned said. He giggled and dashed off ahead with the young ones.

I sauntered along behind and invented stories about faeries hiding in the sparse gum trees, but after a time I thought of Jim. His family lived in the farm next to ours and we'd grown up with them. He worked at one of the other smithies in the village, or used to. There were several blacksmiths in the village, especially after the gold diggings had started in Ballaarat. Jim was eighteen, four years older than Ned and three years older than I was, but only just; I'd be turning 16 in January. He would often walk with us as we took the young ones to school. I remembered the last time he did, when I lagged behind Ned, as usual, he walked with me.

'Imagine how the faeries must feel about Christmas in summer,' I said to him. 'And they'd say you just can't have Halloween in spring.'

'You Irish love yer 'Alloween.' Jim said.

'My family's from near Belfast you know, not Dublin.'

'That's still Irish,' he said tossing stones across the field toward Grant's orchard. 'You know, I don't mind the Christmas in summer,' he continued. 'We can spend the whole day outside splashin' about in one of the rivers. Better than the miserable time my mum and dad talk of about life in England, the freezin' snowy days, with little more to eat than a bit of ham. Here we can have everything to eat for Christmas. Look at this fruit in the orchards.'

'Yeah, I guess so. And I do prefer Halloween in spring,' I said, 'not near as scary.'

He nodded and grinned. His teeth were big and very white. They filled his whole face. Often Ned had laughed at them, but this time I found them cute. I blushed and turned away.

'The diggings. Ahh, 'twould be exciting.' Jim said. He gazed over the road and the sun that dazzled on the yellow fields beyond. 'Soon as I get the chance, I'll be off there.' He turned to me. 'I'd be able to buy ya some fine silk for your dress on our weddin' day, Nellie.'

'Ah, get away with you,' I said and nudged him lightly on the shoulder. I remember the feeling of my hand against his body.

'Ooh, don't push me down the hill. You'll be missing out on the best beau in town,' he grinned at me, pretending he was falling.

We continued on down the hill past orchard trees still in bloom. He reached out and flicked a blossom off my shoulder.

'You know, Bella. I will be doing it, soon. Honest.'

'You'll be doing what?'

'My brother, Richard, is going up to Ballaarat to the diggings and he said I can tag along. We will find the biggest, bestest nugget and we want to find it before anyone else. No time to lose. He has a horse and we will share it. It should not take many days to get there.'

I looked around in surprise. 'But—when?'

'Very soon. Only in a week or so. Richard is almost ready. But Bella, no need to worry, I shall come back for you. I promise. I shall make my fortune and come back to wed you.'

'Oh, Jim. I—'

He took my hand.

'No. Get away with you.' I darted off. Once I'd passed the trees near the lane at the bottom of the hill I turned and called, 'You come back and talk to my Da.' I scurried off down the lane. Jim's smithy lay on the other side of the main road, away from the school.

I'd not seen him since. Halloween had come and gone, but Jim had not returned. I received one small letter, which I hid in my glory box. He wrote that he had arrived in Ballaarat, but had not found any gold. No more letters had come.

Once Ned and I, and the young ones, got to the main road we traipsed along past the smithies, and inns and small shops. The schoolhouse was three miles from our dairy. It lay nearby the other river, the Lardedark, or Lerderderg as some people called it. A small wooden house that the pupils could barely squeeze into. There had been talk of building a new schoolhouse for years but it was yet to happen.

As we continued along some walkers in front of us stopped and pointed into a nearby paddock. Ned scooted off to look.

'What's happened?' Polly asked.

'Looks like a lot of people have camped there over the weekend,' I said, once we caught up to Ned. I could see the remains of some small campfires.

'Black fellas most like,' said Ned.

When we finally came to the schoolhouse the teacher, Mr Morrison, was calling all the pupils in. 'See, Polly, we are late,' I said. 'You must get ready more quickly.'

But Mr Morrison also seemed to indicate for Ned and me to come, along with others who had accompanied the pupils to school.

We looked at each other perplexed. 'Da'll want me at the dairy,' Ned said, but Mr Morrison insisted.

Once we squeezed into the classroom, Mr Morrison hushed us and then began to speak, 'I have an important announcement, which I think you all need to hear. The campfires you have seen on the nearby fields were not from the Aboriginal natives, as some have suggested, they were British troops, from Melbourne. They were summoned to the goldfields to deal with an insurrection—'

What was an insurrection? I wondered.

'—several of the miners had caused a disturbance. It is a very sorrowful story. They would not obey the laws of Her Majesty, and so the troops had to deal with them. Unfortunately, some shots were fired. Several members of the group of miners, I am sorry to report, were killed, as were some of the troops.

'This is an important lesson to us all. We must keep the peace. We must obey the laws of the land. And for you, my pupils, that begins with obeying the rules of your teachers and your parents.

'Now, we shall talk no more of this. I do not wish to hear anything of it from you.'

We all left the room and Ned and I silently made our way back, he to our dairy and I to my needlework classes. I sat quietly all day and Mrs Jones did not speak of the events in Ballaarat at all.

After supper that evening the children went outside to play while Ma and I cleaned up in the kitchen and Da and Ned stayed drinking their tea. Ma and Da began talking rapidly. Da said, 'This thing in Ballaarat was good, not bad. The miners were asking for what they had a right to ask for.'

'But Da, people were killed,' Ma said.

'Yes, they were. That is unfortunate, but that is the fault of the government, not the miners. They are being exploited. The rich are stealing their money. And they have no say in it. Peter Lalor's demands are not just for a cheaper gold license, but the vote! That is what we need.'

'But what has that got to do with it? Why were people killed?' I blurted out.

'Is it a civil war, Da?' Ned asked, somewhat breathlessly. I stared at him. I couldn't believe it, he seemed excited!

Da put down his cup and looked at us both. 'The diggers burned their licenses, because those in power charge way too much money for this so-called 'license'. That's why the Governor sent the Redcoats. The diggers are fighting for their right, our right, to be heard by the Governor, by the parliament of this colony. And not to be ruled by lords and knights and kings, and all those so-called 'squatters'! Those days are gone. We want, we demand, we shall have, democracy!' He took a long sip of his tea, which smelt more like whisky. 'I have heard that a number of our brave diggers have indeed died, but so have some of the Redcoats!'

'But will there be war?' Ned asked again.

'If we get the vote there will not. That will be an end to violence! We won't need violence once we can vote and be heard.'

Ned then ran outside and joined his brothers. They played war games. I went to my room and took out my sewing. What if there was a war? What if Ned had to go into it? What if Jim had been there—?' I pulled my sewing close. I was embroidering a beautiful dress, and continued into the evening under the light of the candle. I would not think about the possibility of a war like the one against Napoleon, nor would I look at the letter that sat in my glory box.

Christmas soon came. It was a warm summery day and Da introduced Ned to the drinking of porter while Ma and I took the little ones down to the Werribee River to play. The faeries in the gum trees watched in curiosity.

The days then drifted past. The sun grew fierce, turning the green grass yellow, and the soil dry and dusty. One Sunday afternoon I went out to the orchard, the trees now heavy in fruit. I stood by the edge of the hill and looked over the road. The diggers had resumed their march from Melbourne Town to Ballaarat. No more troops camped on the grounds near the school, and no stories came of battles in Ballaarat. Maybe the war would not happen.

I looked at the travellers on the road. They all came from the east and headed west; no one was coming from the west.

It seemed like I stood there for hours. The sun burnt into my skin. I told myself I should make my way home, but waivered. Despite the house full of children, it felt lonely.

Footsteps came up behind me. Perhaps one of my faery friends wanted to keep me company, but they sounded heavy, and slow. Maybe it was Ned, or Da.

A hand gently touched my shoulder. I quickly turned around.

'My Bella, my love.'

He stood bedraggled, his clothes dirt-stained and tattered, his boots covered in dust and worn thin.

'I got no gold for you. Not a tiny fleck. I got no food. I got nothin'.'

No one else was about. All we could hear was the squawk of galahs and the warbling of magpies.

'Jim. You are alive!' I threw my arms around his neck and drew myself to him. 'That's all I want.'

He slipped his arms around my waist, and whispered in my ear, 'Would you be the wife of a poor blacksmith's apprentice?'

I held him close.

One afternoon, a little over a year later, I sat in the kitchen with Ma. She began to peel the potatoes for evening stew, but let me continue with my embroidery. Da came in and threw the newspaper on the table. 'We won!'

'What did we win, Willy?' Ma said without looking up.

'We have the vote. Those brave men at Eureka have won it for us.'

I looked up anxiously.

'But there was no war, Willy!' Ma said.

'We didn't need a war,' Da said and beamed. 'Up to thirty of our brave diggers died on that memorable day in '54. Aye, and maybe many more died of wounds. But it went no further. No more need for battles, no need for war. They were heard. The parliament, our parliament, here in the colony of Victoria, have voted to extend the vote for all the men. All of them! Not just those rich squatters, not just the rich merchants, but all of us!'

Ma laid down her knife and looked up at Da. 'It was a hard decision to leave our homeland, to leave our family, our own world, to cross the seas so far away to come to this distant land.' She smiled, 'but I always thought it was the right decision.' Da grinned back.

I smiled too, and continued to work on the embroidering of my wedding dress.

<u>Historical note</u>

The Bacchus Marsh Primary School No 28 was established in 1850 and known as the Bacchus Marsh National School. It was located on the Melbourne Road, near the Lerderderg River; the road that is now known as the Avenue of Honour. When the Eureka Stockade uprising occurred on the Ballarat goldfields extra troops were sent from Melbourne to Ballarat and they marched along this road past the National School. The teacher of the school at the time, Simon Morrison, recorded in his diary the passing of these soldiers through Bacchus Marsh.

Extracts from the diary of Simon Morrison, Head Teacher at Bacchus Marsh National School, 1853-1855.

[Source: Diary of Simon Morrison, located in the Bacchus Marsh & District Historical Society records]

<u>December 1854</u>

2nd.   A large army came to the 'Marsh' today. They are bound for Ballaraat.

3rd. Sunday   The first battle fought between the Diggers and the Military at the Ballaraat diggings. Several have been killed on both sides. Sorrowful tidings.

21st.   The Army returned today from Ballaraat goldfields. Peace is restored.

In 1899 one of Simon Morrison's students, David Grant, also saw these soldiers, and relates the events years later: David Grant, is believed to have been a pupil at the Bacchus Marsh National School between 1853 and 1862. Grant refers to the 'Broadlands' estate, which was not established until 1864, near the site of the old school.

'Mr David Grant said ... he could remember the soldiers camping on 'Broadlands' on their way to Ballarat.'

[Source: Testimonial to Simon Morrison, 1st Sept., 1899, Bacchus Marsh Express]

Daniela Sheen

Having grown up with a love of books and constantly reading, it was only a matter of time before I would also start to write. This is an extract from my first manuscript Purple Dreams, a fictional holocaust story set in the small town of Bad Homburg in central Germany, a few years before the outbreak of the Second World War. Wherever my stories may take me this one is written in memory of my former hometown Bad Homburg.

Purple Dreams

His hands trembled as he lifted the heavy lid one last time to look at the vase with its unusual carvings, the shimmering gold and silver handle, inbuilt gems like fish splattered in the ocean. Saying goodbye to a memory long gone was harder than he thought. The vase didn't belong to him, never had. He never quite understood what had made him take it in the first place and then bury it, but now it was too late; thirty years too late. Whatever instinct, or maybe just greed had motivated him at the time, didn't matter anymore as he wasn't prepared to live with the consequences any longer. He was past all that. Unlike so many other regrets in his life he just hoped this one could be reversible.

Clutching the vase to his chest he slowly got up, shaking off dirt and dust, while listening for possible sounds on the street. The town's people were getting ready to celebrate carnival time, a masquerade ball in honour of the late Kaiser Wilhelm II, who'd taken his summer vacations in this prominent capital of their casino and spa town until his death in 1941. His love for hunting, beer and beautiful women was still etched in their memory, would always be remembered around these regions. Although everything seemed quiet now, he knew that would soon change. It was now or never; the city revellers would be coming soon.

He glanced back down at the spot where the vase had been laying for over thirty years—a deep buried secret he now carried under his arm, wishing to give it back to its rightful owner. A light drizzle began to fall and heavy fog enveloped the mountains beyond, spilling onto the streets; but he ignored it, rushing out the gate towards the cemetery.

He briefly worried what would happen if he was met by the wrong people; not careful enough to instigate the right moment; if they weren't there to welcome him; or worse, if Elisabeth had changed her mind. Discoveries carried risks he might have no control over. His eyes scanned the empty path before him and suddenly he knew that none of these things really mattered, that being there was what counted most. His thick double breasted jacket gave him some protection from the rain as he rushed through the town's graveyard towards the city centre. Row upon row of abandoned gravestones, he was glad to leave behind when he finally stepped outside the curled wrought iron gate, noting the white tower beyond in the distance. Fog drew in closer and faster like milky grey smoke, moving ahead, slowly obscuring the road and trees and houses. Streetlights turned on as if by magic, and slowly, dark shadowy figures emerged like clouds out of nowhere; blurry at first then more sharp, greeting one another.

In the large groups of people along the footpath, who stood alone or together, he searched for her face. Elisabeth. His eyes closed for a second, wishing and praying. A purple light exploded from somewhere and he was walking no longer the cold dirty streets, but found himself inside the big theatre; amidst disaster and confusion. It was 1944. No actors, no performance; just a bulk of hungry or sick people nudging and pushing past him. 'Germans defend yourself,' someone shouted. 'Don't buy from the Jews, gypsies or communists. They are not wanted here.' While others cried out for food, taking whatever crumbs they could find on the floor, he ignored the bouts of nausea, the feeling of de-ja vu arising deep inside the pit of his stomach. What was going on? As he watched the past being played out before him for the second time, the younger, much younger version of himself looked anxiously amongst the faces in the crowd; searching for the woman he had always loved. Where was she?

He got up, eventually. And, just like before, he followed the endless trail of strangers; searching, nameless people too powerless to stop what was happening, who'd lost their flicker of hope, stripped of their rights and possessions, looking for something the future didn't promise. Walking in line behind the others, he knew what was coming even before it happened. They reached the white tower, turning down the small path that led to the castle lake. The drizzle had stopped. Dusk had given way to darkness and mingled with the fog, making it hard if not impossible to see what was in front. In a restrained whisper someone asked for a light—yes, silence was the keyword for survival, without it they'd be lost—and suddenly the edge of the big stone well lay before them.

A wooden bucket fixed with a vigil light was bound by large copper hoops, then hung and lowered inside the well. It seemed forever until it reached the ground, but when it did everyone cheered and clapped their hands. One by one they were lifted down; the sick and elderly, women and children securely strapped onto the thick strong ropes, until the last person was gone. He clutched his vase, refusing to let go. He knew when things had settled down and it was safe again, a train would be waiting for them. Hopefully it would lead them to a better life, a future they deserved. In any case, he would be back in the morning, checking on them every day of the month, until it was over and the last one gone. He turned around, shocked to see her face. Elisabeth. Her dishevelled blond hair and green eyes stood in stark contrast to the dark coat she wore, as did the wet stained cheeks and neck she now tried to hide from him. The strain over the last couple of months seemed to have left a permanent toll on her, nodding and smiling now that she knew he'd seen her—but with a smile that didn't reach her eyes. It pained him to see her like that. And still, so far everything had gone to plan.

In a reflex action he walked up to her, gently touching her face. Showing her the vase he took her in his arms, pulling the hood tighter to keep her warm, hoping it had all been worthwhile and they could finally move on. Her green eyes closed in delight, while tired and exhausted her mouth whispered the words he longed to hear – 'I love you'.

Till We Meet Again

The glowing headlights shone in the dark as the shiny black sedan sped along the wet, bumpy country road; ignoring the speed sign of fifty km an hour, almost doing double the recommended speed limit. It was 1.30am. Light drizzle fell and the light from the three quarter moon cast shimmering water pockets across the car bonnet, running in grooves down the sides, before finally finding its way through an open gap in the window. The woman shuddered at the wheel, goose bumps creeping up her bare arms.

'Uh, close that window, it's chilly outside. I can't afford to get sick.'

Her words were followed by the deep pearly laughter of a man sitting next to her, his long legs only inches away from the dashboard. Smiling, bending sideways, he did as she asked, then said:

'Why are you such a princess?'

Playfully tucking at her coiffed blond curls, he re-positioned himself on the seat.

'Didn't you know that rainwater is good for the skin? It'll make you more beautiful and more desirable to the world.'

'Says who?' She laughed, a little teasingly. 'You?'

'Of course,' he said smugly. 'Who else but your best friend, soulmate and adviser.'

It wasn't as much a question as it was a statement; and she knew it. To her surprise, especially in those last couple of years, he'd proven himself the best friend she'd ever had.

'Well then, let's bring on torrents of rain and showers for my skin.'

They laughed and continued their journey through the moonlit country roads. It wasn't much further now, just one more turn after this one and they'd be home. Driving along, her fidgety hands sought hold of the silver lighter in the handbag between the seats, frustrated that she couldn't find it. They had just left a party in Newtown, a one hour drive away, had spent several hours talking to business associates, movie directors and studio bosses, but now she was looking forward to coming back home again, resting. With her eyes cast down she rummaged through her bag.

'Where's the damn lighter?'

Before he had time to answer her, a large truck swerved right in front of them, without headlights on, zig zagging from one lane to the other. Without thinking she slammed on the brakes, hard and fast, to avoid crashing into it; and in doing so lost control of the car. Silently gliding along the road, airborne with no way of stopping, the sedan spun around in circles, coming to a complete standstill when it hit a tree. The impact was instant and lethal, shook the passengers like dolls in a whirlpool, while the screeching sound of metal still hung in the air. And, like a witness, the screech of an owl sliced through the night, expectantly calling out for a mate, taking with it the secret—and keeping it.

Somewhere nearby, amongst the thicket in the grass, a silver lighter shone in the dark. The locals would later describe it as being the worst car accident in the towns' history, with the newspaper flaunting disturbing images on the front pages. Sadly, for those old enough to remember, it would stay forever etched in their memories.

* * *

Imagine a place of utter darkness for nine months; of movements, sounds and smells shrouded in mystery, living an unknown existence. The gift of life did as it turned from an embryo into a baby, moving flesh on flesh, tiny kicks almost every day; almost certainly a sign that everything was well. No doctors or nurses to check on its progress—just blind faith. A faith that carried fresh hopes deep inside.

At the end of it all the woman breathed a sigh of relief, waiting for the newborn to be cleaned and taken away. Wrapped up tight in a soft warm blanket by a second woman, it was put on a mattress which lay on the floor in the adjoining room. It stayed there for a long time, until she came back again, feeding and changing it. Meanwhile, the birthmother left as soon as she recovered, resuming her duties.

Despite their difficulties, in the following weeks, a routine was established that never seemed to change. When the baby cried, being hungry or dirty, it learned having to wait until one of the woman came back—no choice in the matter—whilst staring into the darkness of the room, in need of the comforting feeling, the warmth of their skin to return. It craved for it, depended on it, at an almost desperate level. Everyday seemed like heaven had opened its gate, as either one held the baby, their love and contentment surging through them like a secure warm blanket.

However, one of the women never stayed long, wasn't allowed to stay—apart from her line of duty—when her eyes always flitted nervously to the clock on the table. She only ever did what was necessary, what she could do, before leaving again. So it became a habit. The baby would be gripped by bouts of loneliness, a fear that awoke him at all hours of the night and day, hoping for comfort from the woman. The touch of her hands became more seldom, sporadic and never in the same order. More often than not there was silence; needs ignored, and cries left unanswered. It didn't know any different.

So the first few months flew by, one by one, days merging into one another, one after the other. As it grew older and stronger, boredom set in. Still laying on the mattress on the floor, it would spend its time tumbling aimlessly from side to side, listening into the silence. Sometimes one of the women would stay, softly rocking the baby in her arms until it fell asleep, singing lullabies and other nursery rhymes in the dark of night. On these occasions there was a special bond of love, warmth and happiness in the room, filling the air far beyond anything else experienced in its short lived existence. Soon the baby learned to differentiate between day and night, feeding and sleeping time, and the women's different routines marking the start and the end of both.

However, even before the first year finished, another change was introduced. A change it couldn't have foreseen, as the night-time woman failed to show up, leaving the baby in its own filth, sometimes for several hours. Hearing them speak in hushed and angry voices the baby felt frightened, less secure in its surroundings, yet wishing to feel the soft touch of their skin. Then one day, it was moved to a different location, a room less dark; one with furniture, a window and a door leading into a garden. It smelled of disinfectant, bees wax and freshly washed cotton sheets. The light was blindingly strong, so bright it had to close its eyes, scared and confused. Again, it was further away, much further, disturbing its routine in a frightening way.

In the same year the women began to feed the child porridge—white, smooth and creamy.

'Here darling,' her soft voice cooed, 'it's a little more substantial than just plain milk. It'll help you grow even more.'

She pulled a spoon from her apron, forcing the strange and unfamiliar food into its mouth. At first, not knowing what to make of it, it turned its head sideways, refusing to eat. Still, the woman didn't give up, and over time, by accidently swallowing a few of the morsels, it learned to enjoy the gluey mix. Content, the child looked at her with wide open eyes, feeling drowsy from the unusual food and the lengthy stay of the woman.

'I'll come back tomorrow. I promise.'

Before she left she pulled a fluffy brown teddy bear from her apron, putting it on the mattress.

'Here,' she said, 'something to hold onto while I am gone.'

Stiff with fear the baby cowered in the corner of the room, watching the unusual object from a safe distance. With the woman gone it soon felt lonely again and, as the night progressed, cold. It began to wonder why the strange object didn't move, inching its way closer and closer. Touching it in a non-threatening way, the toy felt soft and warm against its hand—just like the women's skin. Pleased and re-assured, it climbed back onto the mattress, pressing the fluffy bear close to its chest, then closed its eyes and fell asleep.

Christine Turner

I have always been an avid reader since childhood but have never written anything since secondary school. I retired a few years ago after working in the accounting industry for many years.

My story was inspired by watching a travel documentary and having a very vivid dream the same night. The dream stayed in my head until I was compelled to put pen to paper.

My other interests include calligraphy and I also dabble in drawing and painting.

Ida - Mae

Ida-Mae Watson slowly rocked back and forth in the old oak rocking chair that had graced the front porch of her home for some seventy years. Albert had lovingly carved it for her early in their marriage. Many young babies and small children had been soothed to sleep in that very chair, usually in Ida-Mae's loving embrace, as she crooned soft lullabies in their tiny ears. The arms of the chair had taken on a warm golden patina from those times she loved so dearly. Albert would sit on the porch railing smoking his evening pipe, quietly watching his wife rocking her babies and singing softly to them, his heart swelling with pride and contentment. Albert had been gone some eight years, cruelly taken by a swift and vicious cancer, and not an hour of the day passed when Ida-Mae did not miss him with all her heart. Theirs had been a deep and abiding love.

It had been such a hot day in the dusty Louisiana town just south of the Ouachita River. The weatherman said on the radio this morning that storms were on the way this evening. That would be most welcome as it had not rained for quite some time. Tomorrow is Independence Day Ida-Mae thought idly. She let out a soft chuckle as she realised how many of those she had seen over her ninety-three years although, of course, she didn't remember any of them before she was about four or five years of age. Her granddaughter, Marnie, was calling for her in the morning to take her into town for the Fourth of July celebrations, a parade down Main Street and a picnic in the town square. Ida-Mae wasn't too fussed about going but her family liked to get her out and about as much as they could. Old Doc Simms, who was some twenty five years younger than her but everybody called him 'Old Doc Simms', had only last week increased her angina medication and told her not to exert herself too much, especially in this infernal heat.

Clad in a loose blue cotton dress and her faithful old carpet slippers, her only other adornment was the treasured gold cross another gift from her Albert, hanging around her thin brown neck and the impossibly thin gold wedding band on her finger. The grey, grizzled curls clung damply to her scalp, made even tighter by the humidity of the evening.

In that strange and mystical state between wakefulness and sleep, Ida-Mae took in the familiar night sounds around her. The birds had taken to the trees for the night and the insects took to the air. Mosquitoes and fireflies buzzed around and the moths began their never ending circling of the soft glow from the light bulb above the screen door. Her mind wandered back to the first Independence Day she could remember. It was another hot July day and she was running around with all the other small children in town dressed in a simple cotton dress and barefoot. Nobody wore shoes in those days, most could not afford to buy them and were fortunate if they came by a pair of hand-me-downs after they were well worn anyway. A child wearing shoes, what a luxury!

Ida-Mae was an orphan child taken in by a couple who were unable to have their own babies. Her mother had died in childbirth, far, far too young to be having a baby at fourteen, but those things happened then. The father of the child was unknown, she would never tell no matter what. Lord knows what would have become of her if the Anderson's hadn't taken her for their own. Nobody else needed another mouth to feed. Ida-Mae had a happy childhood she recalled. They might have been dirt poor but her Daddy always managed to make sure they had food on the table and had a roof over their heads. Her Mamma took in white lady's laundry and mending and always seemed to have a needle and thread sticking out of the bodice of her dress. The family attended church every Sunday as her folks were good God fearing people. Ida-Mae particularly loved to sing in church and was an important member of the choir as she got older. People were always telling her what a wonderful voice she had.

One hot June Sunday the church attendance was bolstered by the arrival of the new family who had moved into town a week or so before. As Ida-Mae glanced up from her song-book she saw Albert for the very first time. He was sitting in the back row with his folks, his older brother and two younger sisters. Albert happened to look up at the same time. Their eyes locked onto each other and their fate was sealed. Ida-Mae gave another chuckle as she remembered her and Albert recalling that day, both saying they never had eyes for another from that moment on.

Ida-Mae and Albert married just as soon as their folks would allow, she was seventeen and he had just turned nineteen. Three baby girls arrived over the next seven years, Ruth, Violet and Josie. Ida-Mae and the girls would wait at the front gate every day to welcome Albert home from work. Albert was a carpenter but could turn his hand to anything, fortunately, as there were some very dark times over the years when work was scarce. All things considered, life was good for the Watsons as the girls grew up, married and had children of their own.

Ida-Mae's thoughts turned to all the incredible changes she had witnessed throughout her years, the good and the bad. The wonder of air travel - folks flew all over the world these days and every house had one or two cars. Albert never drove a car, he said he never liked going faster than the few times they travelled by the lumbering Greyhound bus to his sister's home in Baton Rouge. One of those visits was for the family to watch the first moon landing on a television set in the department store window. Fancy that, men walking on the moon! Ida-Mae thought it had taken away the moon's mystery and magic more than being too excited about the event. Space travel, medical marvels and technology had changed the world. Whatever would the future hold?

The dark times surfaced in Ida-Mae's mind. The never ending worry of the Ku Klux Klan burning people out of their homes, the murders, the lynchings, the assassination of a President and a prominent church leader, race riots, and then the awful years of segregation. Those terrible years of segregation had more impact on her children and grandchildren than Ida-Mae had had to endure. It was not quite as difficult living in a small town with a largely black population when compared to those living in the larger towns and cities all over the country.

Wars had taken a toll on their lives too. Albert's only brother John had been killed in Korea, a sniper's bullet had pierced his helmet moments before he had completed his duty watch on night patrol. Albert was heart-broken, his only brother gone. Gone, like so many young men and women who sacrificed their lives in the line of duty. Josie's husband had been wounded in Vietnam and would carry a severe limp for the rest of his life after being fitted with an artificial leg. . . .at least he was alive. Now servicemen and women were fighting in the Middle East in a whole different war, terrorism was now the scourge of the world.

Then there was James. Ida-Mae's heart sank to the pit of her stomach as her thoughts turned to Ruth's grandson James. James was spending the rest of his life on death row in the federal prison in Grant County near the town of Pollock. He was caught, tried and convicted of the brutal rape and murder of his former girlfriend Samantha Brown. Samantha had found herself a new boyfriend, after she caught James out with another girl, and she refused to see him again despite his begging and pleading. James snapped. If he couldn't have her he made sure nobody else would either. He ambushed

Samantha on her way home one evening and her body was recovered, floating face down in the Ouachita River, some ten days after she was reported missing. James had flung the bloodied box-cutter into the undergrowth, after the red rage subsided, and he realised he had almost decapitated her. His finger-prints were on record after a misdemeanour, committed only months before, and, of course, the DNA tests were irrefutable. Shattered and heartbroken, Ruth hardly left her house these days, the shock, devastation and shame inflicted on the family was almost too much to bear. The family all gathered together at Ruth's house on the day of Samantha's funeral, too wrapped in sorrow and grief for any of them to be seen at work, school or anywhere else that terrible day.

As the tears of unbearable sorrow trickled slowly down her wrinkled cheeks, Ida-Mae clutched her gold cross fiercely to her heart, so strongly the cross-bar dug into her frail skin and two droplets of blood trickled between her fingers. She gasped out loud as she felt the pain in her chest spread up her left arm and into her jaw.

Marnie arrived that Independence Day to find her beloved grandmother slumped in the rocking chair.

Ida-Mae's spirit stood at the front gate, waiting, as ever, for Albert.

C.A.Clark

I have always been a story teller; I told stories to the kids who now, apparently, tell them to their kids. I forget what the stories were but they are out there with a life of their own. I started studying writing with TAFE, moved on to Uni for a while and now I use the wonders of the interwebs for continuous learning.

I have had plenty of short, short, pieces aka flash fiction published in anthologies, e-zines, blogs, magazines, and spoken word performance. I enter the odd competition, usually those 25 word or less ones to keep my words sharp, and I read voraciously. I have ideas pounding on the inside of my head begging to be written and threatening my skull's integrity and my rejection folder is beginning to bulge. My favourite book is the dictionary. Everything else about me fluctuates without notice.

Safe Haven

We sat on plain wooden benches in a plain wooden hall. The faint smell of whitewash had many in the group blinking rapidly. The few surviving children clung to their parents. We were a sorry lot, with haggard faces, gaunt from privation, thin limbs curled around loved ones, dull eyes avoiding the glance of others. Many of us clutched battered bags and cases containing our most treasured possessions. One woman held a photo album to her chest. All of us had wounds and scars and grime encrusted our hair and skin. Making it this far past the A.I.s had taken all we had and we were glad for a moment of respite from the terror of the past year.

A group of elderly men stood in front of double doors at the opposite end of the room from where we had entered. They were dressed in plain white or blue shirts with braces to hold up their home spun cotton trousers. The oldest man with a puff of snowy white beard held up his hands to get our attention.

'It will be easier to drag my plough through the eye of my wife's sewing needle than for many of you to embrace our lifestyle.' His accent was thick with Germanic highlights and glottal stops but we understood enough. 'You must leave all vanities behind. All the things you carried here must remain in this room. You must let go of your pride and embrace the joy of our lifestyle. We will not turn you out if you truly wish to stay but be warned, you have three turns of the moon to prove your heart is true. Our life is simple, the work of our hands is clean and in all things we dedicate our labours to the Lord.'

I could hear the capitalisation in his word. He truly believed there is a God; in a world gone mad with AI robots destroying their makers, and all of humanity scrambling through rat holes to survive, this old man still believed in some higher power.

'Let us not belabour the facts. This is the only place left on earth where the mechanical demons cannot enter. To stay here in the relative safety of our home, you must strip off your old life and put on the new. Those who wish to step through these doors must know we will not tolerate disobedience and pride, nor vanity in all its forms. You will be issued new clothing, one set only. If you stay, you will make your own clothing, if you leave, your old things will be waiting for you to take back out into the secular world you are running from. Come now and be welcome.'

Men and boys over twelve and women with younger children were corralled through separate side doors into change rooms and returned cleaner and dressed in plain cotton. Women fiddled with their new prayer caps, hats twisted unfamiliarly in the hands of the men. Everyone looked uncomfortable. Make up and jewellery, including wedding rings, were gone. No denim or spandex, no nylon, rayon or poly-blends, no watches, no hair ties, no scrunchies or high heels, no wallets or handbags, suitcases or backpacks. No phones. No headsets. No computers. All of it stored in labelled boxes on shelves in the change rooms to collect in three months if we couldn't take the change. We had no choice, stay and live, leave and die. Our rag tag group of survivors stepped through the double doors into our new life.

The Last Lecture.

'Young citizens! Today is an auspicious day, a day you have long prepared for. Today is the day when you leave behind your childhood. Today is a day which your guardians and mentors have deemed that you are mature enough and resilient enough to take on your adult responsibilities. This is your rite of passage.'

The auditorium filled with a soft rustling of fabrics as nervous excitement spread around the seated youngsters.

'Your formal education is complete except for this one last lecture. This one lecture will determine your readiness to join the deep dilemma that is the burden of all adults of all the species in all the known universes.'

Silence descended, every set of eyes faced the podium, no one moved. No matter how many times the lecturer delivered this particular final session, it never became easier. Warm waves of reassurance radiated from the guardians, reassuring and supporting everyone present including the lecturer who took a deep calming breath, returning waves of gratitude.

'Imagine if you can, a race, nay a species of beings which has no ability to believe.'

Puzzled murmurs followed the statement but quickly hushed.

'A species which has five physical senses; hearing, sight, taste, touch and smell. Each sense can give an individual member of the species enough information to help them negotiate their world. Some of them have latent, although very basic level psionic abilities. All of them have an aura which acts like a barrier. It is invisible to the majority of the species but it exists as a personal space barrier and has proven to block all access to the mechanics of the species mind.'

The lecturer looked around the seating to assess the young audience. What the lecturer was about to impart would rock them to the core. The guardians, spaced around the upper level of the seating, widened their senses and prepared to catch anyone who needed support.

'Every individual of this species exists in total inner isolation. These creatures cannot sense another member of the species except in the most rudimentary fashion which we believe is due to the aura.'

Several squeals interspersed the collective gasp of horror. A few guardians separated distressed individuals from the crowd and moved them to a recovery area. The lecturer waited until the audience was quiet again.

'There is more you must know. I understand the concept of total separateness is a difficult one to grasp and even more difficult to imagine but you must understand all of this before you can move out of this auditorium. Your guardians and mentors are here to support you. Let others know how you are feeling, how this is impacting you so we can support. The next piece of information is even more difficult. This species lives in a state of complete disbelief. They deny the evidence of their senses, they denigrate information, they minimise and deflect, they scoff at, and ignore, their own experiences and then they wrap themselves in manufactured certainties. They are as unlike any other species in all the known universes and they are supremely dangerous to all of us. Wait, wait, I sense you have many questions but I ask that you hold them until I have finished.'

A ripple of agitation and concern flowed around the room and the lecturer allowed a few moments for calm to settle the fluttering and murmurs.

'These individuals all go through a state in each sleep cycle called dreaming. When they dream, their subconscious allows them to process their daily experiences through abstract images. Sometimes the dream state allows the individual to experience for a brief interlude, the collective consciousness that is denied them during their waking cycle. For a rare few, this gives them a glimpse into their strongest potential future timelines and resonant past experiences. A miniscule percent of them will recall these dream state images upon waking and fewer still will act upon them. The few who do remember usually create what they call, a story. This is where the danger exists. A story is a false narrative. It is what they call a lie. They are the only species known to exist who are able to lie. They do it for entertainment. This however is not the most dangerous part. When they create a lie or story, they tell about the life of someone not in their world. Their story is made up of highlights from another beings life. Not the everyday existence parts but the major turning points in the life of someone. When that person's life is made into a story by this species, they lose all of their memories of those moments.'

Shocked shouts from the students filled the air. 'Impossible!' 'Ridiculous!' 'How can that happen?' 'Monsters!' The lecturer waved for quiet and the guardians reinforced a calming wave to help the young people absorb the information.

'Many eons ago, when the species number was still relatively small, the peoples of the collective universes, tried to influence the development of that species. After many attempts it was deemed necessary to block that world from accessing any other universes and even to keep the species safely on its own planet. The species turned all the interactions into stories so we can only speculate what happened, what we do know is all the beings who went to the planet returned as blanks.

It exists in a bubble, in a universe where all other beings have evacuated to other places. Occasionally throughout their evolution, some have attempted breeding programs hoping that the species could change, or brought individuals out of that world to see if there have been any changes but the individuals are difficult to be around and are quickly returned to their own place. Unfortunately, no matter how many measures we take, they are still accessing our lives through their dreams and turning them into stories.'

The audience had moved into connected clumps, limbs wrapped around each other for comfort. Some openly expressed their horror, fear and distress in physical ways, all were radiating concern and fear. All of them knew of someone with psychic holes in their lives.

'Now there are eight billion of them on the planet. They have begun to explore their solar system. They are sending out probes and searching for life on other planets that they will never find. Their cleverest minds are not interested in space exploration though; they are interested in the connections between universes. They sense there is more than the one they experience. They are still a very long way from understanding the technology and we actively divert their thinking but there is a much bigger problem than scientists. There are more story tellers than ever before and none of us are safe.'

Strong waves of comfort emanated from the guardians but the lecturer knew from past experience that they too were experiencing the grief and fear associated with hearing this information yet again. The lecturer paced across the speaker's platform, clasping limb extensions and building the courage to continue.

'Now is the moment of the great dilemma. This species is completely unaware of what it is doing to the rest of us. Even if they were told, they would not believe it. They will only suspend their disbelief for a story and only while the story is being told, then they return to their state of disbelief. But the more of them who tell stories the more of us are impacted. Any one of us at any moment could become a victim of a story in their world, our own lives reduced to a life of simply eating, sleeping, hygiene and domestic tasks and spending time with people we don't recall meeting or pairing with, children we don't remember having, no memories of challenges or strong connections. Whole civilisations have become victims to the story tellers. Histories, languages, cultures, all gone, only shells left and no way to reverse the devastation of nothingness.' The lecturer stumbled for a moment then faced the audience once more.

'In one week from now, you will be expected to vote. All adults must vote. It must be a majority vote one way or the other. We must decide whether we should ultimately destroy that species to protect all of our lives. Or, maintain the barricades and find stronger and alternate ways of blocking them from stealing our lives. This, my dear young citizens is the burden of adult hood. Now I bid you farewell and ask that you give deep thought to how you will vote next week. Go forth new adults.'

The students filed from the auditorium, blinking at the light as they exited the foyer into the day. Their faces all reflected uncertainty and puzzlement. Many were looking at the sun and back at the building, some were being greeted by guardians and mentors. All were asking the same question.

'Weren't we supposed to be in the last lecture?'

The Bully

My stomach hurt. I had tried to hide in the toilets but she had dragged us all out and stood us in a line in front of the old hall stage.

'Forgotten your uniforms again have you?' The PE teacher sneered at us. The fat, thin, weak and pimply misfits who deliberately left PE gear shoved in some hidden darkness behind their wardrobes. None of us spoke. None of looked at her either.

'Look at me when I speak to you.' she barked at us. Every fictitious sergeant major was channelled through this dictator. She was the physical education tyrant and we were terrified. I could smell hot urine and noticed the puddle before she did. There was nothing I could do and I was just as terrified but luckier to have a stronger bladder.

'You filthy child. Strip off now. You.' She pointed right at me and I jumped, the wet kid was crying. 'Go and fetch the mop immediately.' I took off at a run, so frightened I didn't know where I was running. I opened every door in the hall with clumsy fingers, looking for a mop. Wrenching open a door with a slide bolt, I had a dozen mops and brooms fall on me and I landed on the floor feeling like the bad stick in pick- up sticks. I managed to wrestle the brooms back into the cupboard and dragged the heavy mop back to where my fellow victims stood around the puddle on the floor and I tried to avoid looking at their glowing red faces.

'Put these on.' The teacher threw dull brown material at us. The brown turned out to be large bloomers with puffy legs and matching brown smock tops. They looked ridiculous but we put them on. None of them fit properly. Too big or too small and we looked ludicrous but at least we had something on. One time she had made some kids run around the oval in their underwear. All the athletic suck ups in their pristine sport uniforms with perfectly level socks were jogging primly around the oval when we appeared from the side door. The oval and bleachers were packed with students today and we were the comedy act for a full house. 'Run' she screeched from behind us and followed it with an ear piercing whistle blast. That drew the attention of every set of eyes and a ripple of laughter began doing the Mexican wave as we passed at a shambling trot.

'You,' she screeched at me and pointed a sharp claw into my shoulder blade. I wondered if my bladder would actually hold.

'I saw you run for the mop so don't try to kid me, now move.' The last word was almost a roar and I sprinted away from her in fear she would claw me. Fear can do amazing things to a person and while I was running I didn't have to see the others laughing at me. My face was burning with embarrassment and shame. I hated that woman. I managed to make it around the oval and stopped where she had gathered the good kids. I was wheezing and gasping and bent over to try and suck more air in my lungs.

'We will all do handstands today. Please demonstrate how to stand on your hands for the others, Andrea.' Andrea, 'The favoured one', dropped lightly forward and lifted her perfect legs into the air, balancing neatly on her perfectly manicured fingers and soft, work free palms. She held the pose for several steady breaths then languidly dropped back to her feet and stood up without so much as a hair out of place. I hated her too.

'Simple and elegant, Andrea, thank you. Now the rest of you can try it.' She walked around all of the students and examined their attempts. She praised all her favoured ones, the neatly attired PE prims and berated the rest of us, except me. I just watched her with my anger mounting. She leaned over me, hands on hips and her chin rumpled up in a pug dog fashion.

'Why aren't you doing a hand stand?' I stared her steadily in the eyes and began to squat down. I slid my hands under my feet.

'What the hell do you think you are doing?'

'I'm standing on my hands Miss, just like you told us.' Her face became a purplish shade and she spat as she screamed at me.

'Stand up at once you insolent monster. Everyone gather around. Come and see what this student can do when given instruction.' The others all shuffled over and shouldered into a circle around me. 'Now show them what you just showed me.' I had not broken eye contact with her for one second and I ignored all the other kids as once again I dropped to a squat and slid my hands under my feet.

'I am standing on my hands Miss. Just as you instructed.'

I was enjoying her imminent explosion and hoped it would make her skull burst open.

'Take yourself to the principal at once you stupid, insolent...' her words became incoherent and the laughter that had started as quiet titters erupted to blend with her yelling. It all faded into the background of my triumph. I had bested the beast. They weren't laughing at me. I walked away feeling the slaps on my back from the other kids and I felt good. I basked in the glory of the moment. The aftermath would come and I would deal with it when it did but right now all that counted was the way my shoulders were no longer hunched forward. My chin was up and I proudly strutted away in my brown bloomers to the cheers of the crowd. Chalk one up for the underdog.

Bronwyn Akers

Bronwyn is currently studying for a Masters of Cultural Heritage at Deakin University. In 2015she completed a Bachelor of Arts majoring in History. She aims to have a career in learning and sharing our local history.

Maddingley Park Heritage Tour

Maddingley Park, now in its 133rd year and serving a local population of 18,500, is a far cry from its modest beginnings in 1868; only thirty years after the township of Bacchus Marsh was founded. In this tour we will visit several of the key heritage sites within the park.

During the 1850s the land was the police paddock and also contained Bacchus Marsh's original courthouse (now the tennis clubs rooms). In 1868, the police paddock was re-zoned as recreational and Mr. E Sloss donated additional land, which collectively marked the beginning of the park. At this time the trustee's board was formed, many members of which were Bacchus Marsh shop traders or councillors.

Then in 1884 it was renamed Maddingley Park and a curator employed to establish a pleasure and recreational park. With the establishment of the railway in 1887, Maddingley Park became a go-to destination for many Melbournians for sport and picnics, as it remains to the current day.

Map of Heritage Sites

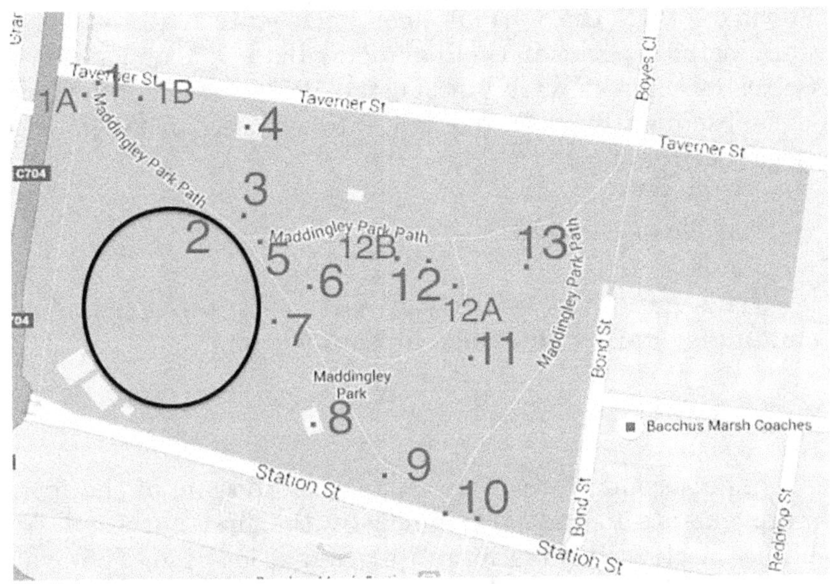

1. Entrance Gates

This walking tour begins at the north-west corner at the magnificent memorial gates. These gates were erected in 1922 by the local branch of the ANA (Australian Natives Association) as a memorial to the fallen soldiers of World War I. The gates were purchased second-hand from the Labassa estate in Caulfield in Melbourne's east. The gates were built in 1880, by Glasgow manufacturer W. MacFarlane and Co., a company renowned for their global exports of pre-fabricated iron buildings. The gates were restored in 2001, after unfortunately being severely damaged in a motor vehicle accident. In 2008 the state government restored the gates again.

1A. Ticket Office

Just behind the gates is the original ticket office catering for all the various sporting events held over the years including cricket, cycling and football. It is no longer in use. Newer kiosks were built in the 1950s for this purpose, but subsequently they too fell into disuse, although the structures remain to this day.

1B. Rose Garden

This garden is lovingly cared for by the Friends of Maddingley Park volunteer community group.

2. Oval

The second site is the sports oval and one of the first improvements to the park made by the first curator, Mr. Johnstone. It still remains in its original location. The oval was and is the location of many cricket and football matches. From 1884 the oval held the annual Boxing Day sporting gala and evening concert, the monies raised were used to improve the park.

In 1895 an asphalt cycle track was built around the perimeter of the oval and then in 1905 the track was further improved. This was used by the Bacchus Marsh cycle club to hold races and cycle events, which again were very popular at the annual sports day.

In 1952 the cast iron palisade fence was erected around the oval that is said to be very similar to the one encircling the oval at the MCG. At this time the oval also became somewhat smaller.

Today the oval is frequently used by local football and cricket clubs and by the Bacchus Marsh Secondary College for their sports days. It is also used for other events such as the Relay for Life in support of the Cancer Council.

3. Sloss Water Fountain Foundations

The drinking fountain was erected in 1888 with funding donated by Mr. E Sloss. The Bacchus Marsh Express, on the 29th December 1888, described the fountain as a small bluestone rock pool sealed with watertight cement with two apartments. Four small spray fountains adorned the front and the pool housed goldfish. Near the path a tap was added for drinking purposes. Today all that is left are the foundations in which a small rockery garden has been created.

Mr. Sloss had a long association with the park when, in 1872, he reached an agreement with the park trustees board to lease the land area for ten years for grazing. Part of the terms of the lease, Mr. Sloss agreed to cut thistles; erect a front entrance, side gates and a three-rail wooden fence around the perimeter; and he was also required to keep the space open to the public. It was through this deal that the trustees were able to clear the land for the park's future designs and plantings.

4. Lawn Tennis Club/Maddingley Courthouse

On the northern perimeter of the park stands the former Maddingley courthouse, built in 1857-58. But it was only used as a courthouse until 1859, when construction of the current courthouse on Main Street, Bacchus Marsh was completed. The sandstones for the foundations were supplied by the local business Matson's Bald Hill Quarry, which also supplied the sandstone used to build Victoria's State Parliament library and Treasury buildings.

In 1866 the building was purchased by the Bacchus Marsh District Road Board, the local authority prior to the formation of the shire council, and was used as their offices. After this, the house was rented out to several road board workers before becoming the residence of Mr. John Johnstone, the first curator of Maddingley Park in 1888. It was subsequently leased to several curators until 1935, when it was finally leased to private tenants. In 1957 it became the lawn tennis clubrooms.

Over the years there have been many alterations and extensions to the building, making it hard to distinguish the original features, such as the sandstone foundations.

5. Shelter Seat

This shelter was originally erected in 1921 to commemorate the women of Bacchus Marsh who organised the Bazaar market and raised one thousand pounds for the park.

In 2007 the Lions Club of Bacchus Marsh undertook a heritage project and rebuilt the seat.

6. Sarah Cafferty Memorial/Former Sundial

In 1889, Mrs. Alford, proprietor of the Railway Hotel, Maddingley donated the sundial for the park. A description of the dial was given in the Bacchus Marsh Express, 10 April, 1899:

A handsome sun dial, the base of which will be six feet in diameter, built an octagon shape, middle in the form of two steps each twelve inches in height, tapering off to twenty-four inches on which a pedestal will stand two feet in height.... On the top the metal dial will be placed.

Today, roughly in the same location now, stands the memorial to the tragic passing of local resident Sarah Cafferty in 2013.

7. The Dickie Bandstand/Rose Garden

The Dickie family presented the bandstand to the park in 1906, in the memory of councillor G. Dickie JP. Mr. Dickie moved to the town in 1853 and started a bakers shop in 1867, before running a general store in his later years. Mr. Dickie served the town for thirty years in various official capacities and was integral to the negotiations that brought the railway to the town. He was an original member of the park trustee board and oversaw many of the parks developments, such as reserving the land for public use and the installation of the cannon.

Surrounding the bandstand is the Nieuwesteeg Heritage Rose Garden. The Garden was established in 2011 and showcases a selection of heritage rose varieties donated by John Nieuwesteeg, who is a prominent Victorian rose collector and propagator. The Friends of Maddingley Park community group also cares for this garden.

8. The Evans Pavilion

The Evans Pavilion was erected in 1896 in the memory of Mr. Isaac Evans, after he bequeathed one hundred pounds to the park's trustee board. Mr. Evans was an early resident of the Bacchus Marsh area, having arrived in Melbourne in 1849, and was employed by Mr. James at the local Broadlands estate. After a stint on the goldfields, he came back to Bacchus Marsh and worked again for Mr. James. After several more years he purchased 145 acres of crown land in the Pentland hills and became a successful stock breeder, winning many prizes at the Ballarat and Melbourne Shows.

9. Gas Lamp

The lamp was erected in 1911 as a memorial to the Honourable George Thomas Dickie. He was a very public figure and served on several town committees and was integral to the Bacchus Marsh Dairyman's Association. He followed in his father's footsteps and was elected onto the shire council. George furthered his political career by becoming the local member of the Legislative Council of Victoria. George passed away at age thirty seven from influenza. Today the lamppost still stands but, unfortunately, it is no longer operational.

10. Pearce Memorial Gates

These gates were erected in 1922 to commemorate the lives of two brothers, Mr. Thomas George Pearce and Mr. Ebenezer Pearce, both of whom served on the Trustees board of the park and were significant businessmen in Bacchus Marsh. Since the 1850s, the Pearce family have run several businesses and the two brothers operated a chaff mill on Church Street, Rowe's Brick works and the well-known chicory kiln, which can been seen by looking down Taverner Street towards the river.

Mr. T G Pearce had a long-standing interest in Maddingley Park and was involved in securing funds for the construction of the fountain and the running of several boxing-day sports galas.

Just to the left of the gates is a single panel of a three rail wooden fence, which has been erected to commemorate (and could possibly be a piece of) the original fence that surrounded the park that was built by Mr. E Sloss in 1872.

11. Lakes

Two artificial lakes were built by Mr. Johnstone and were finished in 1888. Mr. Grant donated a three-foot high cement eagle to adorn the top of an ornamental rock arch in the lake. The lakes were stocked with goldfish and adorned with various plantings including willows, ferns, water lilies and a bridge. It was large enough to sustain a rowboat and had an island that was home to various nesting water birds such as ducks and swans.

At one end of the smaller lake a grotto was built in 1884. The Bacchus Marsh express gave this description:

The other fountain is of a cataract grotto character, at the end of the lake, and is composed of flat blocks of ironstone built up in alcove shape to a considerable height.

By the 1920s, reports in the local paper complained that the lakes were muddy and full of reeds. By the summer of 1950-51 the beds were dry, as one resident remembers running though the bull rushes. By 1967 the lakes had been filled-in with dirt to level the park grounds. Now many of the original trees and plantings have disappeared and very little evidence remains of the lakes locations within the park.

12. Fountain

The former fountain site is the highest point in the park. Today all that is left is a small hill with a flat top where the fountain once stood. Mr. A D Hodgson donated the fountain to the park in 1888. The Bacchus Marsh Express gives this description of the fountain:

The design consists of a fluted vase, wreathed in flowers, standing upon a panelled four sided base, at the corners of which dolphins are placed. The vase supports a circular shell-shaped receptacle for water in the centre of which a female figure stands holding up by both hands above her head a smaller basin in the centre of which a small four headed piece of ornamental work forms the apex of the fountain'.

12A. Cannon site

The cannon, which was situated on the rise near the fountain, was a Sixty Four Pounder gun acquired from the dismantled frigate 'Nelson'. The Nelson battleship had a long life but never saw any military action. It was built in 1814 in Plymouth. In 1860, during the Crimean War, it was refitted with a steam engine but was kept in reserve. In 1868 it was refitted again with forty eight guns, cut down to a frigate and lent to the Colony of Victoria to be used as a drill ship. Then in 1899 it was dismantled by the colony and it was at this time that Cr. Dickie and Mr. S T Staughton were able to acquire the gun, paid for the transportation costs, and installed it into the park. Through its installation it became a well-used prop for photos up until 1939, when the council deemed the base to be unsafe and sold it for scrap metal. There is a remote possibility that when the cannon was sold, rather than being turned in to scrap, it was taken to a prominent location near Kew. It is a mystery that still needs a conclusion so put on your sleuthing-hats, as any more information would be gladly appreciated.

12B. Aquarium Site

Just below the fountain was the location of the Aquarium. Built in 1890, it was a substantial structure with an 8ft by 8ft glass tank. Surrounding this was a 17ft long and 7ft high rock and concrete wall. On the south side was a tank overflow waterfall pouring into an 8ft long rock and concrete basin. A large cave with a 2ft by 2ft mirror was overlooking this pond. On the north side two small rock caves were built, again housing mirrors. On the west side was a second overflow creating another waterfall into a rock cave and pool. This magnificent structure was adorned with various plantings including a variety of ferns such as staghorns. The pools of the rockery contained various water plants and goldfish.

Unfortunately, over many decades, vandals have routinely destroyed many structures of the park including the fountain, grotto and aquarium. As a result of this all the structures and foundations had to be removed from the park over time, due to safety concerns.

13. Adventure Playground

Located at the edge of the former lake, the playground embodies many elements of the town's heritage; including the treed entrance representing the Avenue of Honour, the chicory kiln, grotto, train station and the turrets of the playground representing the ANA building on Main Street. It was built in 2002 over five days by volunteer labour and has been a significant element of the park ever since.

This concludes the tour, but as we finish it is interesting to observe that the park's very existence is somewhat serendipitous. If it wasn't for a few enterprising Bacchus Marsh businessmen, who in the 1860s petitioned for the site to be allocated for recreation, the park could have been the location for a Maddingley town centre with shops and residences surrounding the train station, instead of the very popular recreational space it is today.

My thanks to the Bacchus Marsh Historical Society for their help with researching the information used in this tour.

Brianna Bullen

Brianna is a Deakin University creative writing PhD candidate planning on writing a thesis involving post humanism, science-fiction, neural implants, memory and materiality. Her Honours' thesis focused on clones, robots and art. She has had work published in *Wordly*, *Imagine Journal*, *LiNQ*, *NoiseMedium*, *Verandah*, and *Voiceworks*, and *Buzzcuts*.

A Performance Never To Be Repeated

The National Museum did not know whether to put the performance, already so controversial, in the Science or Arts wing. In a compromise that pleased neither side of the debate, they elected to stage the act outside, erecting a platform in the external juncture between wings. From this stage-body, lit up by astronaut-white LED lights, a system of wires and cameras live-streamed projections of the twin dancers onto a screen behind them. This was for the benefit of audience members in the back rows of the nature square, enlarging the two dancers into giants: doubling the doubles. Detractors had already complained that this staging was contrived to enrage those already disgusted by the clones; they also claimed the decision to stage the performance outside, in full view of anyone walking by, was designed to incite outrage. The conceptual artist responsible for the show—no prototype-clone was thought capable of negotiating contracts, let alone possessing the capacity for choreographic creativity—denounced the detractors as philistines.

The protestors had arrived, with hateful slogans on placards and coffee in hands, forming a barricade at the front of the stage. Security monitored them closely, with guards and video cameras, keeping them behind the boundary-line, a chest-high metal barrier wrapped around the space in front of the stage. The audience-swarm, stratified from the most aggressive protestors chanting at the front through to those merely curious or strolling past at the back, organised themselves in a mostly-civilised semi-circular mass. It was estimated three hundred protestors would attend, and maybe five hundred art lovers, but the numbers were at least double those expected. The park was practically pregnant, swelling with attendees scuffling over paved paths and grass, trying to see the stage.

The performers, androgynous-things in white loincloths, suddenly glided up steps on opposing sides of the stage. As they moved to meet each other in the centre, they mirrored each other's movement foot by foot, hand-sway by hand-sway. Then they stood looking at each other in identical-reverse profile. There was no expression on their faces, the jeers of the crowd unregistered. Linking one arm in arm, twining and coiling them like DNA strands, the clones breathed deeply and faced the audience. The audience gasped: they had expected their eyes to be something unnatural, perhaps red or yellow, but they were newborn blue. Their magnified duplicates on the screen made it easier to imagine the elastic lungs pumping, hidden behind their thin-skinned flat chests. The blue circuit-roots of their veins became prominent as their muscles flexed. Their faces were severe, an effect intensified by their blonde hair being pulled back tightly, styled into singular plaits. Certain members of the audience were already murmuring, wondering if they were male or female, or somehow lacking that part of humanity. Lacking, or less than.

A close observer would have seen how the clones scanned the audience, like machines sifting through trash, looking for the familiar sunglasses of their choreographer. The anti-clone propaganda at the front of the stage had no effect. The more creative protestors had made signs, DIY-constructions in viscera-red, earthly-green and toothpaste-ad white. The signs formed a floating mirage of alarmist hostility:

'Clones will take our jobs.'

'Bloody natural birth, not bloody test tubes.'

'Nothing artful in copying.'

'Think of the environment.'

A young woman's vocally-fried voice extended out of the megaphone in her hand: 'Clones are the excesses of the wealthy; nurture sustainable diversity; make ethical choices.' In time, she dropped the megaphone and pulled out her phone through which to watch and record events.

The clones finally found their choreographer. He was standing at the back of the crowd wearing dark sunglasses, a turtleneck, and smoking a cigarette. His attempts to stand apart from the masses were thwarted in the accumulation of spectators. It was impossible to tell if he was actually observing them or just the chaos, but the clones smiled at each other upon seeing him anyway and began their routine. They let go of each other and widened their stance, identically relaxed and stable. The music dropped, as if from a great height, into the moment. An uncomfortable industrial beat dissolved into an overlay of voices and whispered hisses which caused skin to prickle in revulsion. Meanwhile, the performers jerked and spasmed in synchrony. Then the cacophony gave way to an organ, pleasing and resonant to the ear, and the clones' bodies dilated out, like beauty in a dream, their arms spreading like branches, as if they longed to embrace the audience in their experience. The fingers brushed in the centre in tactile affirmation. Then they swung their arms before them as they loped backwards, their feet skimming over the stage before they stopped. Once settled, they began spinning on the spot with increasing intensity, as the chords of the organ played out louder and louder, before jumping back, recoiling from the explosion of a violin joining the organ. Complimentary sounds swelled together and wounded the audience. The dancers reflected those harmonious but different instruments in their movements,

the one on the left continuing to flow with the organ while
the one on the right jolted with the violin.

The audience stood perplexed, looking for meaning.
They wondered: training or genetic engineering?

The music's crescendo intensified. The clone originally
on the right passed behind the other as they took each
other's positions on the stage. They spun once, twice, three
times in perfectly timed fouettes, stopped mid-spin and
then reversed the direction. The movements degenerated
lower, disintegrating into a series of spins with both feet on
the ground. Their bodies continued to fall lower, and lower,
pulling down onto the stage as if they were whirlpools falling
through a drain. The music stopped; silence broke through.
They fell to the floor, landing at adjacent angles.

Slowly, they pulled themselves up as a voice—no, voices,
their voices—began softly penetrating that silence, a string
of nonsense syllables. They turned to face the audience, their
mouths opening with more human expression than their
blank gazes had previously admitted. The sound, though,
was alien. Then the lip synchronisation failed. Their red-
paper mouths flapped as the audience realised their singing
was in fact a backing track. Perhaps it was their voices, sung
from those lips at a different time—the angelic, genderless
sound seemed to match the faces producing that noise—but
the audience's certainty in their perceptions had gone.

Against the audience's silence, a baby strapped to the
torso of one of the protestors began to cry, causing the mother
to drop her sign: 'Autonomous, not Automatons: Say NO to
Genetic Engineering.'

One of the clone's mouths stopped moving, identifying
the baby and its mother with perplexed eyes. It looked to

its co-performer, who refused to acknowledge the sobs and continued in its out-of-time mime.

At the back of the crowd, the choreographer dropped his cigarette, disgusted at the expressive divergence. Tone was everything; this was the last time he was directing clones. 'Pretentious rubbish,' one reporter had jotted down on his notepad and had not written anything else. Others in the audience were starting to jeer. The noise added an extra layer of discordance to the soundtrack and the performers.

The clones kept going. They ran towards each other from opposite ends of the stage, feet pounding smack, smack, smack, as they gained momentum. One slowed to a stop as the other soared with the music, leaping through the air into its twin's arms. They met in the middle, becoming one being, an organism composed of components reaching as high as it could, and supporting itself to get there. The instruments reached peak harmony. The bottom half spread its legs wide, forming a solid base, and an image of the Eiffel Tower flashed over the screen behind them. The position of the lift changed, as the clone on top spread out its arms into wings, and then curled into a ball, forming the world on its sibling's shoulders as an earth image spun on the projection. It straightened out again and was then swung around, lowered slowly to the ground, putting complete trust in its accomplice. Its bare toes touched the surface, and then once again it was standing beside itself. The violin quivered out one final, fine note.

Then, the soundscape clattered, descending into creaks and screams that convulsed in the air. In unison, from their loincloths, they pulled out sheathed knives. The audience gasped: they wanted their complete erasure, but not their deaths. For several seconds startled pandemonium rippled through the spectators like an electrical current. Yet no one said a word. Were they going to die for their art? Was their art merely a symptom of death? Their director turned away from them, shaking his head, as he left the vicinity.

The clone on the left ran the knife down the skin on its left arm. They had become distinguishable, one bleeding, the other whole. The audience gasped again. Then the clone on the right did the same to restore their identical identities. They switched each other's spaces on the stage, circling each other and slicing—only skin deep—one slice at a time in identical places. Differentiating then dissolving. Differentiating then dissolving. With one final slice, and the sound of fabric tearing, their loincloths fell. The clones stood to face the audience. Tattooed, from pelvis ridge to ridge, was the phrase, 'We are humans. Do you fear yourselves?'

Art on the body. The body as art. The audience screamed in fury. The clones had been created infertile. They had no right to such a display!

Security stormed inwards to hold back the incensed crowd.

A tinny voice echoed from the stage. Or was it two voices speaking slightly out of time? 'Thank you all for coming to watch our performance today.'

The clone on the left spoke, flicking his arms to remove the excessive blood. 'We truly appreciate it, my father and I.'

The other clone gave a paternal smile, wiping the blood from his son's/brother's/self's arms. Both dripped, red on white, bleached further by the stage light.

The beer cans the crowd threw at them conveyed the message to cease more eloquently than their garbled words ever could. But the clones carried on.

'We've always wanted an outlet to speak to you all—

'But we've never had the chance.'

'We find your discourse about us—

'Has been too one sided. We are grateful—

'To have had this opportunity provided to us—

'We wanted to open up—

They were the last words to be heard, as the frenzied crowd rushed the stage to complete this last wish.

April Mullins

April is a 45 year old mother of two, who has lived in the Marsh for eleven years. She currently works on checkout at Foodworks. She is also a Visual Merchandiser who has worked in art directing, prop making, choreography and managing fashion and designer stores. Her belief is the present time is the most important time. Having worked in many fields she finds that the most rewarding thing to do is caring for family. Writing is her release from the daily grind.

Stranded On This Island

Innocence is gone
Locked up, with Captain Cook.
SORRY for invasion.
We did not know that then.
Embarrassed with the knowing
That we felt, to take it in.
Take more than we could give;
Sow or raise or grow.

We see the error of our ways,
Strive to make amends.
Nothing can change it back
We are stuck here
On the Is-Land, girt by sea.
Colonists' cornucopia: glee.

Learn to swim or sink, they say,
Make it the Home-Land.
Took what we thought was free,
As colonial eyes best see.
We cannot give what was not ours.
Stranded on the Island.

Mother Land won't take us back,
Convicts did their time.
We did the best we could.
None of it was done alone.
We cannot give it back,
Dirt we will never own.

We are a melting pot.
Sometimes we feel alone.
So many different nations
Welded to this blazing spot.
We do not know who we are
Or figure what we've got.

Indigenous Australians, and
Torres Strait Islanders:
Hold your heads up high.
You will always be
The only truth we cannot deny.
You belong. We are just
Stranded on this Island.

Teepee Dreaming

STARSHA

I don't know where I am. I thought I went to sleep but now I am suspended, between the worlds of today and yesterday. Looking at yesterday it is nothing like what I recall. I am not in Flinders Street, Melbourne in my father's office where I crashed for the night. I am in a teepee somewhere in America. How did I get here? What is happening? Why am I wearing these clothes? I will just trust, just go with it and see where this leads!

In my bedroom I stare up at the stars, animal hides the height of three men on the wall meet at the stars. Magnificent wooden posts like crossed fingers give strength, a random patchwork of slate carefully smoothed and secured with hard clay. I look at my hands—they are more tanned. My skirt has fringing at the bottom and it is made from some sort of suede hide. I see One-Claw has left the bearskin rug too close to the hearth again. (Who is One-Claw?)

Sitting on the cold worn stones, I sweep grey ash off the fire pit, awaiting his return. I brush with delicate strokes across the grey stones, caressing the ivory handle intricately carved with zig-zags, the cool smoothness of the leather binding, entwined around the horse-hair brush in my hand. Bristles sweep elegantly across the large flat stones worn by generations of use. Sheltered by the glow of the fire and the sheer size of our tribal teepee, the scent of burnt sage lingers in the air, all the leaves are removed and the stone is clean, ready for One-Claw to come home from the hunt. The men were away just one week and the shaman tells me that One-Claw has seen a spear, I will have to tend him on his return.

Worried about the depth of his wound, pondering the magical day that the shaman gave me the gift. Healing heat and the vision, seeing to heal the health of others, feeling blessed beyond belief; yet this may be why we are not with child as our function is a greater purpose to the community. One-Claw and I have been together many moons; our childhood of playing by the stream together progressed to a pure love that nothing could break. Learning to live together came easily to us. Seemingly not just on this earth for ourselves, we see the true shining beauty in nature.

Picking up the ivory handle and placing it back beside the burly bearskin rug that warms us by night. Lying down gently on the rug, I stare at the angle of the teepee, thinking how the tunnel towards the sky is so vast. I recall pretty blue gemstones and white sage that I was given to heal others, its smoke that was brushed around my body for purification. Suddenly I hear Shanty cry out in happiness at the return of White Feather; so I know any minute my One-Claw will be home. I rustle my hands through the bearskin rug, and go to the fire to stoke it, ready with water in the hanging kettle drum. My heart flutters as I see his rugged reflection on the drum.

One-Claw walks over close and holds my hips as he smells my hair. The scent of lemongrass I washed through it this morning. The smell of his sweat hangs like a heavy fog and I turn slowly to see blood on his forehead. Gasping at first, I see it is only a slight nick.

'A Ho, enchanted one,' says One-Claw

'A Ho, my love, O let me see.'

'We have named your brother Short Arrow, as he may not be trusted with anything more.'

Cleaning his wound, I gently brush his fine hair that is falling softly against his eyebrow. It falls gently over his lean shoulders. One-Claw closes his eyes tight and curls the corners of his mouth, as he breathes in gently. I absorb his love, as he sits completely at my disposal. Running my fingers gently in lines from his temple to his chin his breath continues, as if sleeping, so I ask, 'Do you like that One-Claw?'

'Hmm, a yes,' is his response, eyes still closed.

Kissing his smooth voluptuous lips gently. He opens his eyes and dissolves into me. Starting with a tight embrace.

Then I wake up next to Jamie, my brother, with his Doc Martens in my neck on our father's couch. 'Oh you little shit, why wake me up, I was having a dream?'

'Yeah, I know. But if we don't get the next train we'll be late for Nan's birthday lunch and mum will kill us.'

'When's the next one?'

'Twenty minutes.'

'Let's bolt. You got the keys to the front office?'

'Yep!'

'Oh, thanks for that.'

We bolt for the train and I wonder what that dream is all about, then I look across and see a crow. 'What's a crow doing in Flinders Street? That's odd!'

'Who knows?' says Jamie, as we make it to the platform just as our train is pulling in.

Two guys get out and one pulls out a knife. Jamie pushes it away in a mad scramble, but clips my temple with it. I feel my chest beating faster, tasting blood on my lip, then everything goes orange and I fall to the ground...

JAMIE

Jamie yelling, 'Starsh, Starsh...oh wake up, Starsh.'

The ambulance driver pushes past me and then the world goes slow. Everything is in slow motion, I can't believe what just happened to my sister. I look up at the ambulance driver and they ask if there is anything that they can do for me. 'Is there anyone we can call?'

I say, 'That's my sister. I have to call Mum and Dad. We have missed the train and they will be worried.' All of a sudden it is like we fast forward, like I have been frozen to the spot for hours.

The ambo says, 'look mate, you're in shock. Let's just stay sitting down, while we find out what hospital your sister is going to.'

Shit, shit, fucking shit! Mum is going to KILL ME, it is my fault, I kept Starsha out all night.

Oh no! Nan's birthday lunch, no way. Nan, Mum! Oh, I feel sick. Oh, Starsh, wake up...

Oh God, she has to be all right. GOD, if you exist, please help me. I know I don't ask you for anything when times are going good, but if you help Starsh get better, I might just do something about that. I will be so grateful. I have to tell her she is the best sister. I have never told her that. I am an asshole, I always rib her about her alternative clothes and music, but she really is the coolest, most awesome, rad sister a guy could have.

Oh this sucks, Oh what a fuck up. Oh she has to be alright.

What happened to those dick heads? Who stabs somebody they don't even know?

(The police radio confirms the guys have been caught at the local pub—Markillies—on the corner of Flinders and Spencer Street, selling stolen goods on the premises.)

The day is definitely looking up. Dad swings by. The ambulance driver has given him a call from Starsha's phone and he is standing on the platform looking worried over Starsha on the gurney. He comes over and gives me a gigantic hug.

'It is okay, Son. Just stay here a minute. The ambulance driver is taking Starsha to the Royal Melbourne Hospital. Your Mum and Nan are on their way.'

'Oh No! This has ruined Nan's Birthday,' I say.

'You sure didn't ask to be stabbed today, I am sure,' says Dad with a grin.

'It is more the knock on the head they are worried about, the knife was just a graze.'

The ambo comes over to me so I stand there. They check my eyes and say I am in shock and I can't go to work for a few days.

STARSHA

I am not awake but I can hear what is going on around me. The nurse is talking to me, telling me what she is doing, that I am at the Royal Melbourne Hospital. I have had a knock to the head and will be alright—when I wake up. My parents are on their way. I heard them come in. I heard Jamie say, 'Oh so sorry Starsha.' I try to say it is alright, but I can't wake up. Then I fall asleep again. I can't feel anything. I wake up, but I am not here, I am back in the teepee.

One-Claw has a bleeding head and I wash it with the skins and water I boiled on the fire-pit.

He kisses my lips and I pull my hips away, as he tries to grab my backside.

'Star, what no like?'

'I worried you exert yourself, One-Claw.'

'Come here, my woman.'

'We have ceremony, we must hurry.'

Beat, beat, beat…my heart.

Beat, beat, beat… (The sound of drums) dripping like a tap.

Beat, beat, beat…We are sitting outside the Teepee.

Beat, beat, beat…The dust flies up from the skins as they…

Beat, beat, beat…

One-Claw, Shanti, White Feather, Short Arrow.

My kin is all I have. ...they sit cross legged around the fire,

As they beat, beat, beat... the love in my heart glows.

Looking around the circle, beat, beat, beat.

The orange glow of the fire on their faces. Beat, beat, beat.

Black Crow stands up says, 'Spirits see such sadness, they want to see smiles. I pass on the ways of the Great Spirit. On your day to day dealings, smile and be kind. The world is gentle, you just have to look at the flowers and the trees. They slowly stand up amidst the breeze they reach for the stars and the gods. Be like the flowers, be gentle, there are many ups and downs. The seasons change, just know that, just as bad weather has been, good weather will come again. After the rain comes the growth of the grass, the flowers and the trees. The birds will sing again and you too will sing. Great Spirit has changed our life to be easier. We now have carts to carry, containers to gather and all is provided to sustain life. You can see and communicate with the world of spirit. Spirit gives you answers when you ask, then listen.'

'It is easy for spirit to cross back to you. It is you who feel it. You may have the smell of smoke, flowers or a song come to you and you know that spirit is with you. You are spirit, you have a body, but without the body there is no spirit. Spirit is not just for people, as animals are spirit too. Honour your spirit, as spirit honours the temple of your body.'

'Great Spirit says we are here to learn, some to be family, some to be lonely, some to be healers, others to be warriors. Some to take the extra shot with purpose, like

Short Arrow. (Everybody laughs and looks at Short Arrow).
Short Arrow has learnt to control his temper, while you all
tease him. Look back into your past and see where you were
going to be, in one direction. Has your direction changed?'

'Friends, true friends find you again. Spirit has the
finger on the button. Keep a smile on your face for everybody,
as you don't know how much others might need to see one. If
there is anything you need you just have to trust and until
next time Black Crow says thank you, for giving me your
special time and we appreciate you listening.'

Beat, beat, beat go the drums. We look around again to
the smiles and laughter, as the dancers circle around the fire
with painted faces. Then we follow and join in. It is a joyous
day.

My fingers tingle and my head is spinning and I talk
and people can hear me this time.

I wake up in hospital, everyone is there from the
ceremony. They were all in my dream.

Jamie looks so sad.

'I want to see smiling faces,' I say.

Then I realise I have heard that somewhere before.